MW01264528

L I F E
in the
LAND
of the
LIVING

Daniel Vilmure

L I F E
in the
L A N D
of the
LIVING

ALFRED A. KNOPF
New York 1987

THIS IS A BORZOI BOOK
PUBLISHED BY
ALFRED A. KNOPF, INC.

Published in the United States by
Alfred A. Knopf, Inc., New York, and
simultaneously in Canada by Random
House of Canada Limited, Toronto.
Distributed by Random House, Inc.,
New York.

Portions of this work were originally
published in *The Harvard Advocate,
Padan Aram: The Harvard Literary
Review* and *Red Beans and Rice*.

Library of Congress Cataloging-in-
Publication Data

Vilmure, Daniel.
Life in the land of the living.

I. Title.
PS3572.I39L5   1987   813'.54   87-45101
ISBN 0-394-56142-2

Manufactured in the United States
of America
FIRST EDITION

TO MARCUS SMITH
AND
BOBBIE BRISTOL

Nothin' feels better than blood on blood.

—BRUCE SPRINGSTEEN

L I F E
in the
LAND
of the
LIVING

He was dead set against me going, but there was nothing he could do.

I sat on the bed while he watched me. I put on one sock, rolled it up to my knee, then rolled it back down to my ankle. Then I did the same with the other.

"Hand me my shoes. They're right there on the dresser."

"You can put on your shoes if you want to, but you're not going anywhere. You might even ask me to hand them to you, and I might even do it, but that won't change matters none."

I looked at him and through him and past him to the shoes.

"I can get up and fetch them myself if you're too lazy to fetch them for me."

"If I'm too lazy to fetch them for you, what does that say about the one who wants them fetched?"

I got up and went to the dresser and took the shoes. Then I sat on the bed and looked at him while I put them on.

He said, "I'm leaving now."

"So long."

He bit his lip.

"If you come after me," he said, "I'll kick your ass."

I already had my shoes on.

"You don't scare me none."

"I should."

I stood. When he went to leave I went right with him. I hung right on his heels.

"I'm warning you."

We passed down the hallway, through the kitchen, to the utility room. He paused on the lip of the back-porch like a little kid pushed to the edge of a diving board.

"I'm going now."

"All right."

"I'm going now and you're heading back inside."

"We'll see," I said. I looked at him. "We'll just see."

He stepped down, took five paces into the yard, and turned to face me. Then I stepped down, took four steps toward him, and did not flinch when he swung. I was up from the grass in plenty of time to take the second punch. It landed harder than the first and a wetness spread across my lips. This time, when I hit the grass, I did not get up, and when I did get up, some time later, I lay on my daddy's rollaway bed with a brown paper bag full of ice on my jaw. I was bleeding. My brother said, "There's some mercurochrome on the nightstand." Before I could get it he took it up and tossed it to me. I dabbed it on my lip and watched him pace back and forth in the halfdark. He hugged himself with his own hands. "Always has to have his way. Stubborn as a girl.

Jesus Christ, should've knocked that look clean off of him. Should've shown him who's boss around here."

"Shut up."

His jaw dropped and his face froze deadpan. His undershirt was covered with some of my blood and in the yellow light of the backporch he looked like a clown with a knife in his back.

"What did you say?"

"I said shut up."

"That's what I thought you said."

He took out a cigarette and lit it and smoked it. Then he blinked and turned pure red and tossed the cigarette down to the floor. He leapt. His face came to hover not one inch over mine. His cheeks twitched like lizard tails.

"You're lucky I haven't killed you by now. You're lucky your guts ain't strewn across the living room wall."

I imagined that, imagined him stringing my guts like tinsel all across the living room wall.

"Will you get off me now? I'm tired of bleeding on you."

He rose with one swift push and went and stood by the bedroom window. The curtains ballooned about his head and he looked like a spirit through them. In the pocket of his army jacket he carried a canteen. He said it was filled with medicine and no one else could drink from it. He reached into his jacket, took the canteen, unscrewed the top, and took a short swig. Then he coughed and held his hand to his chest and caught his breath. "Stuff tastes terrible," he said. "I'm telling you."

I asked him for fun what the medicine was for.

"Helps the blood circulate."

He reached into his breastpocket and took out another cigarette. He stuck it in his lip and let it dangle there. I did not know if he was going to smoke it or wear it.

"I think I stopped bleeding."

"Good," he said.

His eyes grew narrow and he put his hands on his hips. He was still staring through the open bedroom window.

"What are you looking at?"

He did not answer me. He took a long drag from the cigarette and wiped his nose with the back of his hand. He blew some smoke through the wirescreen.

"Hey. What are you looking at?"

He motioned with his jaw. "Bellamy kids."

I rose on my elbows. "What are they doing?"

"I don't know," he said. He sniffed and leaned hard against the windowsill. His head fell below his shoulders and he crossed his legs. Beneath his undershirt his stomach rose and fell. He looked dead tired. "I don't know," he repeated. He did not look up. "Playing Statues, I guess."

I got up from the rollaway and went to the bathroom and dumped the ice in the bag down the sink. Then I went to the window and stood beside my brother. He was five years older than me, and I could barely see above the windowsill, but he took me up on the tops of his shoes, and then I could see fine.

Through the wirescreen, past the backlot, and over the dogworn chainlink fence, the Bellamy children had gathered around the lopsided base of a tetherball pole. From the screenporch the sound of a piano came, and

whenever the music stopped, so would the Bella-
mys. They looked like they were having a good time.
Jerry, the youngest, mimicked a gorilla. Jeanne, his sister, crouched like a crawfish. Leslie, clearly, was a
squatting baseball catcher. And Thomas, who was my
brother's age, lay stretched out like a dead man.

My brother said, "He's too old to be playing games
like that."

A ribbon of smoke crawled from his mouth.

"Still," I said, "it's a pretty good statue, don't you
think?"

My brother brought me off his shoetops.

"Depends," he said. "Depends."

We left.

The cars were coming home from work as we walked
down Pennymont Boulevard. You could tell which ones
came from Martis Mechanical and which ones came
from Dheu Southern Chemical on account of the condition they were in. Martis cars had greased streaks and
rust stains, worn-out tires and fender-bent bumpers.
Dheu South cars were in better shape, long and sleek
and smooth-running, and each was covered with a fine
cake of phosphate.

The drivers were like their cars. You could tell
who was who by the shape they were in, too. Martis
workers chainsmoked and bounced to the radio and
waved at one another through rearview mirrors. But
Dheu folks sat behind the wheel stonestill, never looking to the right nor the left as if the world on either side
scared the absolute hell out of them. It was curious.

I called to my brother.

"What?"

"Watch this."

I turned my back to the traffic and unbuttoned my pants. Then I mooned the world.

"Jesus! You *pre*vert!"

He grabbed me by the scruff of the neck and hustled me over to a mobile home villa. He brought me behind a clump of ixoras and ordered me to button my pants. I could hear all the cars on Pennymont honking.

"Jesus!" my brother said. It was the second time he'd said it.

I snugged my pants up around my hips.

"What?"

He knelt down and took me by the shoulders and shook me.

"What the hell'd you go and do that for?"

I looked at him.

"I don't know," I said. "I suppose I wanted to see if they'd notice."

My brother threw up his hands.

"Why hell yes they'd notice! They would and they did! Don't you never ever think?"

I glared at him. He glared back. He didn't need to talk to me so bad. I was thinking when I pulled my pants down. I wanted to see if the Dheu South workers would notice. I wanted to see if they weren't as dead as they looked. Besides, if a fella wanted to take off his pants, I supposed he had a right.

"Well," I said, "did you think it was funny?"

He looked at me helplessly.

"I'll tell you what I think," he said. "I think you got both wheels stuck in the sand."

He slapped me on the side of the head and led me
along till we were back on Pennymont.

I could see the LB&T.

It was almost six-thirty.

The Losian Bait & Tackle Store sat in the dead center of
four billboards. Its walls were made of corrugated tin
and its roof was made out of green seethrough plastic.
Come rainy season my brother and I would climb the
palm trees beside the store and drop down onto the plas-
ticoated roof. Below us the shapes of men would move
slowly, and before us pools of polliwogs lay. We'd take
off our sneakers and scoop scores into them, then lower
the shoes down onto the ground and walk home barefooted, prizes in hand. In our backyard a bathtub brim-
ming with rainwater made a fine home for the tadpoles,
and we fed them twice daily on a strict diet of crushed
cockroaches and maple syrup. We put a hurricane
board across the tub to keep the frogs from jumping out,
but that wasn't a problem. In the darkness their eyes
grew as big as wiffle balls, and fattened up by maple
syrup they ballooned to a shape more round than long,
like fleshy heads of dead cabbage with stublegs and
bugeyes. But they were good-behaved and never caused
trouble.

Some we sold to a science teacher and others we
liked we kindly set free. A few, however, were not for-
tunate.

I came home once to a sink full of Bud cans and
bloody legless frog bodies. A saucer of cooking grease
sat by the stove and an unsettling smell hung in the air.

"Nice and sweet!" my daddy called from the dinner table, bleary-eyed, his jaws working. "You boys shore make a good frog!"

I threw up.

To some degree the owner of the LB&T resembled a frog. His skin was so pale as to appear green, his cheeks bulged permanently with chewing-T that might have been flies for all my brother and I knew, and the flesh about his face and body hung in surplus pouches. His name was Lester Losian, and he spoke like a frog would could frogs speak: slow and graveled and godawfully deep. And you could barely see his lime-slice eyes for the mole-covered lids that bunched up over them.

Once my daddy told me that Lester Losian made more money leasing out space for his billboards than on any bait and tackle he might have sold over the counter. Lester himself had informed our daddy that the only reason he kept the store open was because he loved to fish, and because he respected fishermen, and because it was "a fisherman's duty to work toward the preservation of a dying sport."

"And so you realize," our daddy explained, "that the LB&T remains open solely out of the goodness of Lester Losian's heart."

Of course Lester's heart didn't keep him from selling bait at cutthroat prices, nor did it knock out of commission the only Coke machine this side of the county that asked seventy-five cents a pop, nor especially did it call to a halt those Saturday night, all-nite poker tourneys—the ones that kept Lester independently wealthy, the ones that progressed complete with jungle juice and potato chips, the ones that followed my daddy headbent into a confessional and hellbent through his Sabbath day drunk the very next

afternoon. And so Lester was as much to blame as
Bohannon.

Dewey Bohannon had seen me walking down
Fulbright Avenue the afternoon of that same day. I was
alone and a good mile from home, and he pulled his
milktruck up alongside of me and coasted slow.

"You! Boy!"

I did not answer him.

"You! Little feller! I know you can hear me!"

I started to walk on the inside of parked cars, hoping
he was following so close he'd crash. But he didn't.

"You! You!"

"What is it?"

He said my mama's name. She was with him then.

"You her boy, right?"

"I am!" I hollered. "And I'm also my daddy's—
more his than hers! You can have the old bitch for all I
care!"

At that he parked his truck, got out, and started to
run. I ran too. I ducked into a construction site and
stopped dead at a puddle of mud the size and depth of a
swimming pool. I waded in up to my neck. When Bohannon came upon me he fingered the fabric of his uniform
and circled the pool like a displaced shark. His bald head
and black eyes burned in the daylight.

"You come out of there!"

"You go to hell!"

He took out a dollar bill.

"I'll give you this!"

"And I'll give you *this*!"

I displayed a mud-covered middle finger. He was
none too pleased after that.

He started circling the puddle faster and faster, like

the tigers in the Sambo story. After a while I thought he'd turn into a tub of butter, but no such luck. He stopped and caught his wind and wiped his face with a wrinkled bandana. Then he pointed at me and his finger shook.

"Listen, you, I'm gonna say something whether you wanna hear it or not, and whether or not you actually do hear it, it's up to you to tell your daddy what it was that was said, and who it was that said it, and why it was he said what it was he said. You got me?"

I started to laugh and swallowed some mud.

"And don't you go funnin' me!"

I laughed harder and swallowed more mud.

"All right," he said. "Laugh, then. But listen." He began: "There's something your daddy owes your mama and me. He knows what it is, so I don't have to name it. We've been waiting plenty long for him to give it up, and we're not going to wait any longer."

I didn't know what he was talking about.

"Tonight," he went on, "at six-thirty, I'm going to be at the LB&T. Now I know your daddy's going to be there, so don't you try and tell me he ain't."

I wasn't going to tell him a thing.

"Oh, yes," he said. "I'm on to your game before you can play it!" He scratched his head and collected his thoughts. "Yesterday," he continued, "your mama and I went downtown and got us a court order to collect what your daddy owes us. You hear that, boy? A court order. Judge says there ain't nothing this side of hell, your pa included, that can put a stop to such truck as that. Tonight I'm gonna bring that piece of paper with me, show your daddy we mean business. And if he don't want to see it, if he puts up a fuss, well—I'll make him see it!" He wagged his finger at me again, stubborn, like it was some sort of Sears and Roebuck mail-order wand. "So you can just tell him that! You tell him all I said! And you also tell him to make sure he doesn't decide not to show up, 'cause if he does, I swear I'll make it twice as worse for him! You follow?"

I didn't say a thing.

"Good," he said. "Tonight, then. Six-thirty. You tell him."

He turned and left. As he was walking away I scooped my hand in the pool and nailed him in the back with a cake of mud. He shot around and considered me hard and the veins on his forehead pledged allegiance. He looked like he was working up the nerve to kill me, but he decided against it. "That's all right," he said. "I can change uniforms. I'll forgive you this time, boy." And he left.

That was when I ran home and told my brother and he decided that we shouldn't tell our daddy. Instead, we would be there for him; that is, my brother would be there for him—it was before he had decided to let me go.

My brother didn't know either what it was our daddy owed.

Coming on six-forty-five, Bohannon hadn't arrived. We sat on the steps of the LB&T listening to country music playing inside. Every now and then my daddy's voice rose above the clamor of the poker players, either in a drunken cackle or a born-luckless groan, as if he'd just been told a good dirty joke or else been dealt another lame hand. Come seven we were sure Bohannon wouldn't show. He was nowhere in sight, and we sat there watching heat lightning gather its children in the sky. I was just about ready to suggest we go when we heard it: the cry from our daddy, the noise of tumbling boxes, the sound of chairs being drawn to the corners of the room. We looked around. Bohannon's truck wasn't anywhere; maybe he had walked. But how had he gotten into the baitstore?

"The backdoor," my brother whispered. He took me by the shoulders. "Listen," he said. I could hear them inside. "You stay here and pound on the door until they open it. If you pound long enough, well, I'm reasonably sure they'll open it for you, then you can come on in and help Daddy. But not until they open it, you hear?"

I nodded and began to pound. My hands grew raw to the sound of my daddy getting whupped. Two or three minutes passed and the noises grew louder, the bumps against the walls and floor more ferocious, but no one would let me in. Through it I could hear my daddy's voice, then my brother's, then Bohannon's. All the while the men in the store shouted "Get 'im!" and "Good 'un!" and "Sumbitch!" Their feet scraped against the floor like hooves of animals. When I heard Bohannon's voice quit and the backdoor slam and the slapping sound of running feet, I knew the fight had ended.

I crawled to the back of the LB&T, hopped the kneehigh picket fence that separated the frontlot from the back, and stepped through a curtain of vines to the porch of the backdoor. It was flung open, and yellow light poured through. All I could see was my daddy, facedown in a puddle of vomit, and every now and then he added a little to it. My brother sat on top of him like a lifeguard pumping a drowning man. He held him tight around the stomach and made sure every ounce came out.

"Come on, now." My brother's face was bleeding. He pulled tighter at my daddy. "Come on."

The men stood in a semiserious semicircle around the two of them, a little too ashamed or amused to watch, but far too curious not to. Some smoked cigars and others stood with their hands folded across their bellies, discussing it quietly amongst themselves like you might discuss the obvious outcome of a prizefight. Lester himself sat fatassed on his jukebox and blew a ring of cigar smoke as thick around the middle as a glazed doughnut.

"Ever see so much puke in your life," he said, "or what?"

My brother looked at him and spit on the floor. Then he hugged my daddy hard around the midsection and every last bit came out. It swept across the floor in a sour wave and the smell wafted up to the aluminum rafters. The men in the store grimaced and headed for the Coke machine—sixbits for a settled stomach. I kept my eyes on Daddy. He commenced to spitting and lipsmacking and clutching the air with his hands, like he'd just been awakened from a lifelong dream. His eyes blinked furiously.

My brother took a handkerchief from his jacket pocket and rolled off of Daddy. He cleaned Daddy's chin and face and neck. There was blood and plenty of it beneath the vomit, and my brother wiped all that away too. When he was done I walked over to him and looked at his undershirt. Where once was just my blood now was mine and my daddy's and some of my brother's. There was also a good bit of vomit, but I didn't look at that.

A fisherman entered the scene with a cold glass of water in his hand. He brushed it against his chest and forehead and looked at my daddy.

"You know your son went and saved your life?"

Daddy looked at the man, then he looked at my brother. He brought his fist as hard as he could across my brother's face.

"He's no son of mine! He's no goddamn son of mine!"

My brother did not wait to start bleeding, nor did he bother to look at who hit him. He ran.

I was up after him.

The last thing I remember seeing of my daddy was him flat on his back staring at the ceiling, at the overhead lamp which swung in the air like a tethered bird. Lester had just handed him a cup of something, and he had just taken it. "Good medicine," he said, tasting. "Good, good medicine."

My brother fled to the old marina across the road from the LB&T. It had gone out of business years ago and it looked like the carcass of a gutted fish.

One red light lit the boatyard. It hung on a wire from a tall metal beam and swung in the wind like a copper pendulum. The light cast shadows the color of blood across the frame of the deserted hangar, and the water from the harbor made a clicking noise against the empty docks.

All the boats were gone, all of them—the runabouts and motorcrafts and polished overnighters, the royal yachts and cabin cruisers and pinshaped hydroplanes. Once, for the space of three days, our daddy owned a pram. Then he sold it.

In the sky stormheads gathered and heat lightning rose and spread and collapsed. A sixthsensed humming filled the air full and the wind seemed to whistle with newborn force. In the harbor the blackcloth of the water wrinkled now and again with white flowers of foam, and old rusted boatyard pulleys clanged against posts like terrible bells.

I didn't know when the storm would come. It might wait until morning, cut loose with the next heard drum of thunder, or might not come at all. There was no way to be sure.

I'd followed my brother out the backdoor of the LB&T, had followed him running through six lanes of traffic, and it'd been a virtual dead heat till we reached the row of barricades blocking the entrance to the marina. That was when I remembered what it was I had forgotten—that my brother did not run, he flew. And when he saw the barricades assembled there before him, he did not fly, he exploded.

I tried to keep up with him but realized it was impossible. For every footfall of mine I heard, two more of his fell fully unheard. He took the barricades like bushleague hurdles and hurried past them into the docks. In all the humidity my breath came in clouds, and I stared at the night—it had hid him in its pocket.

Already it was dark, dark and falling darker, and I could not see to see. When I entered the hangar which rose above the docks, the brewing storm hung in the hollow like a hymn. The hangar was a remnant of an old abandoned airfield, and the marina had been designed so that in the event of a hurricane boats could be hauled up high on pulleys and left to rest within the shelter of the structure. For this reason the docks stretched halfway beneath the hangar and halfway out into the harbor.

The structure itself was big as a cathedral. Stepping footfirst into it was like stepping footfirst into the body of a man. The walls were made of a white peeling metal that looked like skin, and the ceiling was supported by a series of crossbeams curved in the shape of a collapsed ribcage. On either side of the hangar, docks jutted out from long narrow spaces that glowed like wet wounds.

When I came to the last of the glowing spaces I heard my brother's voice. It rose in a low melodic moan and seemed to blend perfect pitch with the wind. I ducked my head beneath a beam and saw him sitting at the far end of a dock. His jacket, shoes, and undershirt lay folded beside him, and his face was buried in the carriage of his knees. His hair tossed in the wind and his body shone with darkness. He had his hands wrapped about himself, as was his habit, and his shoulders rose and fell in an attitude of sadness.

He looked at me.

"I'm your brother, ain't I?"

He stood and touched his clothes with his toes.

"Listen," he said. "I'm your brother, ain't I?"

I nodded.

He smiled and swayed and pointed across the water.

"Meet me over there."

He dove in.

I watched him for a while. Then I got his things. I would meet him on the other side of the harbor, on the shore by the road. I did not know if he would make it.

———

I waited. I had his clothes folded in my arms. Ten minutes had gone by. I figured in the time it took to walk to
where it was he said he'd be, he could've crossed the
harbor twice and back. So if he wasn't there by then, he
must've drowned, and if he wasn't drowned by then, he
should've been there. And he wasn't there.

I didn't pray because I didn't know how—at least
not yet. That was the same night Number One taught
me. He knew all kinds of prayers—the Hail Mary and
the Our Father and the Act of Contrition. He also knew
over one hundred bad words, some in different languages. They were easier to remember.

The time I found the two of them together Bohannon had used a bad word, one even Number One didn't
know. It had shocked my mother. She tugged the bedcovers up around her neck. "Don't talk like that," she
said.

I stood there staring. Beneath the blankets, I supposed, both of them were naked. I had come home from
school early. It was George Washington's birthday.
That made it halfday.

"Hello, honey," my mama said.

I could tell she was trying not to cry.

"Hello."

Bohannon had his face buried beneath the pillows.
Maybe he was trying not to cry too.

My mother kept looking from him to me and back
again. Usually when I came home from school on a halfday, she'd have lunch waiting for me. This time she
didn't.

"Have you eaten, sugar?"

"No'm."

"Promise you won't tell Daddy about this."

"I promise."

She looked at Bohannon and her lip began to tremble. When he took the pillow from off of his head, she let out a little cry and punched him in the shoulder.

"Hey!"

I didn't know his name was Bohannon then. To me he was just the milkman, a man who'd been around as long as the garbagemen, my daddy, the neighbors, or anybody. He used to give my brother and me free pint cartons of Borden's chocolate milk. He liked to give my mother two sticks of oleo for the price of one.

"Get up, goddamn it!" my mother shouted. She practically kicked Bohannon out of bed—No, she *did* kick Bohannon out of bed. He landed on his rump and let out a grunt. "Get up and put your goddamn pants on!"

Bohannon looked at my mother sideways and shook his head. Then he stood up, rubbing himself.

"That's one tough mother," he told me.

I stared at him, and my mother screamed.

"You shut your mouth! Shut it this instant! How dare you talk that way about me with my youngest boy around! Don't you have any sense? Don't you have even the least amount of human pride?"

Bohannon surveyed himself.

"Not at the moment," he said.

He began to trudge around the room, looking for his trousers. He couldn't find them anywhere.

"They're over there on the vanity!" my mother cried. She buried her face in her hands and I went and stood beside her, though I shouldn't have. She looked up at him. "Oh, you! Oh, you!"

He knocked a couple of things over.

"Where'd you say they   "

"On the goddamn vanity!" she hollered. "For the love of decency, get out!"

Bohannon waved his hands and waggled his jaw and zipped up his trousers. He had found them.

"Don't worry," he said. "I'm getting. I'm getting."

By the time Bohannon had dressed completely, my mother stood beside me. She'd somehow managed to slip into a nightgown and apply fresh lipstick and rouge to her face. She was a hard person to figure out.

Bohannon made to leave and she cleared her throat. He stopped where he was. She walked over to him, not looking at his face, and took him by the arm and led him over to me. She smiled, weakly.

"Before you leave," my mother said, "I would like for the two of you to meet each other." Then she added: "Proper."

"For the love of Christ," Bohannon said.

She stared at him like she might chew his head off. He quieted.

"Son," she said, turning to me, "this man is Dewey Bohannon. He is the milkman." Then she turned to Bohannon. He was smiling. "Dewey," she told him, "this is my son." She looked at the both of us like she wanted us to make nice.

Bohannon wiped his nose.

"Hey, little cowboy."

He stuck out his hand.

"Hey," I answered.

I did not take it.

When he left through the frontdoor and climbed in his milktruck and drove with a shot down the street and away, I took my aluminum baseball bat and broke every unbroken window in the house. I saw Mama take a piece of the glass and look at it and put it in her pocket. That had happened one year ago.

One week after it happened, our mother, my daddy's wife, moved out. But I still saw her all the time.

She got a job working the cash register at the Winn Dixie on Clairview. She'd give me free gum and crap whenever she worked the candy counter, and now and then she'd stop me on the way through and tell me to look after my daddy. She seemed happier than she'd ever been.

One day I walked through the express lane where she was working with a whole package of Little Debbies tucked beneath my T-shirt. She winked at me and smiled and made like I better hurry the hell up so she wouldn't lose her job. So I did. When she smiled I noticed something I'd never noticed before: my mother had the most beautiful teeth.

Fifteen minutes had passed and my brother still hadn't shown. The storm had blown over, as most summer storms do, but the water in the harbor tossed and collided just as violently as before. I considered calling the Coast Guard, but didn't know exactly how to go about it. Then I considered diving in after him, but figured why sacrifice two lives for the sake of stupidity? After a whole half hour had passed, I dug a cross in the sand with the knob of my toe and stood up and started home. Halfway down the shore I came upon him.

He was kneeling behind an oleander heaving to beat my daddy, and his face was still bleeding. That was my family all over—blood and puke and puke and blood. I tapped him on the shoulder and he cast a backward glance in my direction. His face was covered with sand and stray green threads of bile. He looked like he'd seen the face of death itself.

"You all right?" I asked.

He coughed up another bucketful.

"Hey," I repeated, "you all right? You gonna be all right?"

He tried to answer and got tangled up in his own heavings. I thought I could make out a "What?" somewhere in the middle of his misery, so I asked the question again.

"I said you gonna be all right?"

He grabbed whiteknuckled on to the branch of an oleander and did not turn around as he shouted. "I just swallered half the goddamn ocean! I'm bleeding," he hollered, "like a stuck puh-pig! No, no! I'm not goddamn all right!"

I watched his shoulders arch up. He was all right.

It was coming on eight, well past suppertime. We had no money, no fishing poles, no desire to return home to an empty pantry. I had the feeling we were going to be out until morning.

"Where are we sleeping tonight?"

"Wherever we want to."

My brother started to skip in place. He looked like a boxer.

"Can we sleep on the railroad tracks?"

"We can if we want."

We crossed the intersection at Pennymont and Gambril. There were less cars. We passed a Texaco station, the Bullseye Bar and Grill, the South Pennymont

Nursery, and a Salvation Army dumpster. It drooled clothes and shoes.

"Can I look?" I asked.

"Shore," my brother said. "Help yourself."

I ran to the dumpster, used a weatherbeaten love-seat as a stepping stool, and snagged myself a nice pair of corduroys. They were red flares. I wrapped them around my neck and ran back to show them to my brother. An old man in a passing car called me a son of a bitch.

"Do you think he'll call the police?"

"Yes," my brother said.

He took the red cords from around my neck and inspected them. He held them up to the light of a streetlamp and brought them to measure against the length of my leg.

"These are too short."

I looked at them.

"Even for nigger pants?"

"Even for nigger pants."

Without asking my permission, he let the cords drop into a puddle of ditchwater. They soaked it up quickly and stained black. As I walked away I wondered who would find them in the morning; I wondered whose they'd been.

A train of thunder moved across the sky. My brother craned his neck, then he brought his head down and shook it.

"Listen to that," he said. "Will you just listen?"

He lit a cigarette. I could tell he was getting hungry on account of all he was smoking. He'd gone through the better part of a halfempty pack in the last halfmile.

"You're going to get cancer," I told him.

He wagged his head sadly. "Boy, do I know it."

With that, my brother swung around in front of me and held me in place by the shoulders. He looked into my eyes and grinned, and his cigarette shook on his chapped lip. "Watch," he whispered. He tossed the cigarette down and produced another magically from behind my right ear. He lit it and held it burning in the darkness. When the cigarette had got itself going good, the back of my brother's throat clicked and the round hole of his mouth spouted funhouse music. He placed the fresh cigarette in between his lips. "Lungbuster," he proclaimed. In the space of twenty seconds he dragged the cigarette down to its nub. He coughed for round about a minute. "I suppose I shouldn't do things like that," he said.

We were walking again.

It was humid. My skin felt like a suit of rubber and sweat ran through my pants and undershirt. In all the dampness my brother'd gotten weak and he rested on my shoulder—halfwalked, halfleaned. He looked like something from another world. His jeans were stark blue from the harbor water and he must've been chafing on account of his cowboy walk. His hair licked up and out in every direction, disheveled by waves and set stiff by salt water. And of course he was bleeding. There was no end to it.

"You all right?"

"I am."

He peeled a halfmoon of dried blood from the apple of his neck.

"What do you mean asking that?"

"Well," I said, "you're bleeding, and everything."

He stopped leaning on me.

"I'm always bleeding."

It was the truth. I gnawed at a fingernail.

"I know that," I said, "but you're bleeding more than usual."

He picked up a rock and hurled it at a passing car.

"Not really," he said.

From the direction of the road there came a shattering of glass. We heard brakes scream and cursing and the sound of honking horns. My brother turned a whiter shade of pale than he was already.

"I had no idea—" he began, and his eyes followed the wounded car as it made an illegal U-turn. "I didn't mean to throw it so hard," he said.

The car pulled off the road and onto the pavement where we'd been walking. It eyed us for a while as we stood in its headlights, then the motor kicked in and it barreled toward us. We could see gravel kicking up beneath its wheels.

"Holy shit," my brother said.

He told me to get out of the way, which I did, but he himself didn't move. My brother stood what ground he had, and the car seemed bent on getting even. It did not honk or flash its brights, and the driver didn't wave a warning hand; it just barreled on. I called to my brother to get the hell out of its way, but he wouldn't listen none. He acted like he didn't give a damn whether he got run over or not. Let the driver get blood on his car, he didn't care. And it was probably the casual way he handled the whole affair that saved him. As the car sped nearer and nearer, he took out a cigarette and lit it and smoked it and stood staring into the oncoming lights. He even tossed the cigarette down halfthrough, reached into his jacket, and lit another one. He had the routine down. When the car applied its brakes at last and slid a narrow inch from my brother's beltloop, he looked over at me and grinned, as if to say, "See? See? That's how you do it." He also flicked ashes on the hood of the automobile, for effect.

We couldn't see the driver of the car, but we were sure he could see us. Beneath the tinted glass of the front window, a hand reached over to lock the cardoor, and at the sight of my brother lit bloody in the headlights, the vehicle put itself in reverse and sped backward into the blackness. I could see the broken glass web of the back window, but I couldn't make out the driver through it. It might've been a man or a woman; it might even have been a kid.

My brother stretched out his arms at his sides.

"Hey," he said, checking himself out, "am I that gruesome?"

I didn't say no.

In a while we stood across the street from the Stop 'n' Go we planned to get our supper from. There was only one attendant, a beer-bellied redneck with eyes like dull matches and a three-day beard. He stood behind the counter leafing through a magazine. Every other page he'd stick his paw in a bowl of cordial cherries beside the register.

My brother laughed. "This shouldn't be too difficult," he said. "But I think we're going to have to try something different."

Usually how we did it was we both went into a store at the same time. One of us would strike up a conversation with the cashier while the other filled his pockets. It wasn't awfully impossible. This time, however, my brother was in too sad a shape to remain inconspicuous. We both knew we had to come up with a whole 'nother routine.

After some time thinking my brother rose from the curb where he sat. He took off his army jacket and helped me into it. I was almost lost in the thing, and before he handed the jacket over he was careful to remove the canteen from it.

"I'll take care of this," he said. He shook the canteen and I heard the medicine jostle. "Now you listen carefully." I did.

When he was in position on the side of the store nearest the traffic, I gave him the sign and went flying into the Stop 'n' Go.

"Mister! Hey! You've gotta help me!"

The redneck let the magazine slip from his hands and leaned over the counter, playfully.

"Keep your pants on, tiger. What seems to be the problem?"

I acted as if I couldn't catch my breath.

"It's my brother, mister! He's been hit!"

"Been hit?" He leaned closer. "Hit by a what?"

"By a car!" I cried, grabbing at the counter. "He's been hit by a big ole car!"

The redneck made a sour face. "A car?" He shoved his hands in his pockets.

"Yeah!" I told him. "An auto-mobile! And he's dying! I drugged him over to the side of the Stop 'n' Go here so they wouldn't get him again." I held up my hands; there was some of my brother's blood on them, and the redneck's eyes seemed to kindle a little. "Would you come see him? Oh, he needs help plenty bad!"

The redneck chewed the inside of his cheek and looked to either side of him and brought his chin to rest in the cup of his hand. "You better not be fooling me," he said.

"I'm not," I lied. "Boy Scout's honor!" I did something or other with my thumb and pinkie finger, and the redneck seemed impressed. But I'd never been a Boy Scout in my life. I'd never even seen one. "Come on, mister, quick! He's dying!"

The redneck drew a deep breath and took off his work apron. He tossed it in a corner and trudged out from behind the counter. Then he stared down at me. I could barely see his face for his belly.

"Now I'm gonna go look at your brother," he said, "see if I can help." He pointed to the glass doors. "What I want you to do is stand there. Don't move, for one thing, and don't let anybody in, for another. Is it a deal?"

I nodded.

When he was gone I went to the deli section and took four sandwiches. Then I went to the drink aisle and got a bottle of Gatorade. We could share it. I also got my brother a pack of cigarettes, because he'd like that, and a brown bottle of mercurochrome, because he needed it. It didn't take me but thirty seconds to get everything I wanted, because I didn't want much, and all of it fit nicely in my brother's army jacket. By the time the redneck came out from around the side of the store, I was standing guard how he'd told me. The redneck looked like he'd seen a ghost.

"He all right?" I asked. "He gonna be okay?"

"I don't know," the redneck said. "He's awful bad."

On cue, my brother moaned. A chill seemed to spider up the redneck's spine.

"You get the license plate number of that car?" the redneck asked.

"No," I said. "It was going too fast." I looked at the redneck. "Hey, mister. Aren't you going to call an ambulance or something? You ain't just gonna let him die there?"

The redneck ran a hand around his stubble and tried to grin a toothy grin, but his face fell all apart in the process. "Jesus!" he shouted. He slammed his fist into his hand and squatted down before me. He had breath like a catbox smells.

"Listen, darlin'," he said. He was sweating regular bullets. "I've got to mind the Stop 'n' Go. That's my job. It's all I have to do. I'd like to help you, but company policy says I can't." His face was red and he looked ashamed. "Now I can witness your brother dying. I can do that for you if you want me to. And maybe I can even lend you a dime out of my own pocket so you can phone an ambulance yourself. But as far as making your brother better, I can't try a thing. I can't move him, nor touch him, nor prop a pillow underneath his head, nor do one dog-helping thing to him. And that's the God's truth. If I did, little buddy, this here Stop 'n' Go might be held legally liable, and you know what that would mean?"

"What?" I asked him.

He bowed his head.

"I'd lose my job."

With that, my brother moaned again. It was a terrific moan.

"But he's dying!" I cried. "Can't you even hear him?"

The redneck looked at his catcher's mitt hands, stood up and folded his arms across his chest, and said he was very sorry. He disappeared into the Stop 'n' Go, breathing sparsely.

I brought the sandwiches to my brother.

"What took you so long?" he said. "Couldn't you hear me moaning?" He moaned again and laughed. It was a pretty decent moan, I had to admit it.

"I'll be right back," I said.

I got up and walked around the corner of the store and stood there staring through the glass front of the doors. When I walked in, the tinkling of the bells nearly gave the redneck a heart attack.

"What!"

The magazine in his hands trembled. It was a wrestling magazine.

"Mister," I said, "I don't think my brother's going to die."

"That's good," the redneck said.

He did not look at me.

"Goodbye."

"Goodbye."

As soon as I left I went back in.

"Mister?" I said. "Could I have that ten cents you said you'd lend me for an ambulance?"

He looked at me and nodded slowly, then he put his magazine down and searched through his trouser pockets. I went to the counter and watched him. He emptied the contents of his pockets out before me and separated the coins from the lint and cordial cherry wrappers.

He had nine cents to his name.

"A penny short," he mumbled, sadly. He stared off into the distance. "A penny short."

I looked at the cash register. He saw me looking at it.

"Is that a cash register?"

He studied it for a moment, like it might have been anything.

"Yes," he said. "Yes, it is."

"Is it yours?" I asked him.

He shook his head.

"No. It ain't mine. It belongs to the store."

"Oh," I said, not looking at him. I took the nine pennies and arranged them in an incomplete circle. "Does the cash register have any pennies in it?"

He nodded his head yes. He was a very honest man.

I looked at him.

"Can I have one?"

"What?"

The question seemed to stagger him.

"Can I have one?"

He steadied himself. His eyes went dull and glossy.

"Son—"

"Just one?"

I looked at the incomplete circle.

"One?"

"Only one."

He clenched his teeth and gathered his will.

"Son, I just . . . can't."

Turning away, he shuffled over to the other side of

the counter and pretended to straighten the dirty maga-
zines. I watched him for a while, not saying a word, and
as I left I slipped a couple of Slim Jims in the pocket of
my pants.

"Don't worry!" I shouted. "He probably won't
die!"

I wanted to reassure him.

The Double D was cheap, but cheap is never free.

"Two dollars a carload," my brother whistled. He
lay on the side of the Stop 'n' Go with a copy of the day's
paper in his hands. He'd found it in the gutter and it was
filthy with gutter water. "Two dollars," he repeated. He
was surrounded by broken glass and cellophane sandwich wrappers. A bottle of Gatorade tottered on his
stomach. "Mmm, mmm, mmm. That's cheaper than a
worn-out mop."

He was feeling better. Stripes of mercurochrome
covered his face and he looked like a painted Indian.
Beneath his army jacket his stomach bulged. I supposed
he wasn't hungry anymore.

"But we don't have a car to drive in with," I told
him. "How we going to get into a drive-in without no
car to drive in with?" I didn't even mention the two
dollars we didn't have; I didn't say word one about
them.

"We don't need a car," he said. "I just ain't sure I
want to walk all that way if it ain't going to be a worthwhile movie."

"Can't you find the listings?" I asked.

"I've got them in my hands, don't I?"

That didn't answer the question. The problem was

my brother couldn't read the first or last half of the American alphabet. The only reason he knew it was two dollars a carload was because he could see the big "2" with the dollar sign next to it on the advertisement in the paper. He also knew it was two dollars a load because every Saturday the previous summer our daddy'd taken us to the double feature at the Double D. We'd sit in the frontseat while he fell asleep in the back, and if he were still out by the time the movie ended, my brother'd get to drive us on home.

"Hand me that paper," I told him.

He did. I scanned the listings.

"The Double D," I read aloud. "Cleanest and most beautiful drive-in theater in the South. Tonight, James Dean revival. At eight o'clock, *East of Eden,* followed by *Giant* at eleven. Two dollars a carload. First come, first serve."

I looked at my brother. It was like somebody'd told him he'd just won an all-expense-paid trip to heaven.

"Come on!" he cried. He tore off.

I must have gotten there about fifteen minutes after him. It was a long run and I had short legs. I saw him standing by the redclay road that led to the box office. A sign was posted in the ground beside him: "Deadheads will be prosecuted." Deadheads was slang for people who snuck into movies without paying. My brother and I were deadheads, or at least we were going to be. It was only a matter of time.

A long column of punk trees separated the Double D parking lot from the rest of the world, and the peeling punks were held in line by a tall barbed-wire fence. Through the brush we could see the weedpocked cement

lot with its rows of rainbeaten radio speakers, and already
a bunch of folks had gathered. Some sat crosslegged on
cartops drinking beer, and others sat buried in frontseats,
exchanging Junior Mints, popcorn, and preliminary kisses.
At regular intervals station wagons and lightbed trucks
loaded down with ten or five or fifteen kids would speed
past my brother, leaving him to cough amid a claycloud of
red dust.

He saw me. "Pah—what took you so long?"

"It was only about a thousand mile run," I told him.
"Why didn't you slow up?"

He scratched his ankle with the toe of his shoe and
waved his arms in the boiling dust. "I didn't want to be
late," he said. "You got to learn to set your feet to my
clock."

We started walking toward the box office at the dead
end of the Double D road, which was nothing more than a
wooden shed with a dusty plastic screen, lit from within by
a blue revolving buglamp. The usherette in charge was
pale and poorfed with eyes the color of wet lumber, and
we stood in the shadows so she wouldn't see us.

My brother turned to me.

"You ever seen a James Dean movie?" He asked it
like you might ask someone whether they'd ever tried glo-
rified rice. "I ain't never taken you to a James Dean
movie?"

I looked at him.

"Who's James Dean?"

We snuck around to the punk trees that grew beside
the box office. My brother gave me a leg up and we began
to climb. The dying wood flaked from the trunks like
reams of faded wrapping paper, and when we reached the

uppermost bough of the tree my brother took a deep breath and leaned hard outward. I got nervous; we were pretty high up.

For conversation I asked him what was so great about James Dean. My brother spit and it stretched to the ground.

"Well," he told me, "he's the coolest, for one thing. And in *East of Eden* he's just like me."

"How come?" I asked. His answer came quick.

"'Cause his father hates him and his mother's a whore."

My breath fell fast. I looked at him, hard.

We hung about five feet from the platform of the box office, shrouded in a quiltpatch of moonlight and leaves. Just as my brother was about to make his move, a man in a white station wagon came driving down the clayroad. He was curious as to what we were up to, so he pulled to a halt and flipped on his brights. "Christ!" my brother said, diving beneath some foliage. "That son of a bitch want to get us killed?" I thought we were done for, but nothing happened. The man dimmed his lights and drove on through.

My brother sighed. "Come on, now." We dropped onto the platform and nobody heard us.

For a few moments we lay there. There was a nice wind and the air smelled like melted butter. From the box office below us rock 'n' roll played, and the usherette kept herself company singing. After a while I turned over. My brother lay with his head in his arms, and I stared at him.

"Take back what you said."

He didn't answer.

"Take it back, goddamn it. Take it back about her."

He stood and stretched and scratched beneath his arms.

"Be quiet," he told me. "Another car's comin'."

He crouched down low and a long dark Cadillac with a makeshift sunroof pulled up soundlessly. I peeked over the lip of the platform and saw a twenty-dollar bill pass from the car to the box office window.

"Wait while I get your change," the usherette said.

We heard her exit through the backdoor and saw her walk across the lot to the concession stand.

"Now it's time," my brother told me, putting a finger to his lips. He stepped from the roof of the box office to the Cadillac cartop. The automobile sank a bit, but the driver inside did not notice. My brother stretched himself lengthwise and with absolute silence, and his face came to rest above the unopened sunroof. He held out his hand.

"Come on," he whispered.

"You go to hell."

"Come on, you idiot."

"I ain't comin' with you."

He held out his hand a little bit farther.

"Come on," he said. "Come on, now. Please."

Without knowing why, I crossed to the cartop. I lay down beside him and we were very still. Beneath our shirts I could feel the engine rumble. I heard the voice of the usherette and the sound of money being peeled and counted. "Five, ten, and three is twenty." The car started to move and I opened my eyes. Below us I could see the shapes of two people. One was a man and the other was a woman. They were not moving or talking and the radio wasn't on. They were just sitting. As the car pulled into the Double D lot I looked at my brother. He was taking a long drink from his canteen and when he finished he closed his eyes and water flowed from them. We came to settle in the final row of automobiles, far separated from the other cars, and I lay on my side against the sunroof. It was very hot and my brother lay with his shirt up over his head. If I strained to listen, I could hear him whispering.

"She's not a whore. She's not a whore. She's not a whore. She's not."

The movie began.

"Please."

It woke me.

"Please."

I didn't know what it was.

"Please?"

I was dreaming.

"Please?"

I wasn't dreaming.

I looked at my brother. He was dead to the world. I looked at James Dean. He was sitting on a ferris wheel. I looked at the cars. They were gray and silent. I didn't know where the voice came from, then I heard it again.

"No! Please? I told you nice. Not *here*, not *now*. *Please?*"

I looked through the sunroof of the Cadillac. Two shapes moved. One was on top; I could see his back. The other was on bottom; she made the noise. She, the one on bottom, had her hands around the wheel; white in all the darkness, they were all my eyes could see. He, the one on top, arched steadily faster; curving like an instrument, he made a curious music: unkind, unnatural, a sad, forced thing. As his head bumped hard against the glass of the sunroof, I was surprised he didn't wake my brother with all his crazy commotion; I was surprised she didn't wake

him too with her godawful moaning; and I admit I was
tempted to wake him myself, just so he could have the
opportunity to see them, but soon they slowed their
rocking-horse rhythm and their bodies relaxed like a run-
down toy. He curved upward and fell straight off of her,
and her hands around the steering wheel unclenched from
white to black. Silence passed while he sat shotgun, fid-
dling clumsily with the fly of his pants, and she lay beaten
beneath the upright wheel, not talking, not moving, not
seeming to breathe.

I put my head down. I felt spent and unclean. I
looked at the cars on either side of me, then I stared again
through the fogwet sunroof.

She had moved her hand to the part of the steering
wheel where the horn was located, and her other hand had
followed suit. Slowly and completely, like an oyster surrounding a single speck of sand, she closed her entire body
about the wheel. The horn blared. The man took a fright
and tried to pull her loose, but she clung to the wheel and
shook her head, screaming, "No more! No more!"

My brother awoke. "Jesus, Joseph, and Mary!" He
tumbled to the ground from the top of the car.

Headlights flickered on around the Double D lot
and folks headed over to see what the excitement was
about. I rolled off the top of the Cadillac and landed beside
my brother. Together, we watched the people gather.
They walked quickly, as if they were in danger, and behind them on the big screen James Dean was busy beating
the absolute crap out of his brother; there were punching
noises on the radio speaker and punching noises coming
from the inside of the car. My brother's eyes were blood-
rimmed and centered somewhere far away. It seemed he
was still sort of halfasleep somehow.

"What the hell did you do this time?" he asked. He asked it like someone sleeping asks something.

"Nothing!" I shouted.

"That's even worse!"

His hands twitched at his sides and his voice was very panicky. He slurred many of his s-words.

"So you ain't reshponshible?" he said.

"No," I told him. "No, I ain't responsible. I just watched."

He studied me with a cocked eye, poked me in the chest.

"Watched what?" he asked. "Watched what!"

"Them," I said. "The movie, I mean." I turned my head away.

All the while the horn kept roaring, and the inside of the Cadillac came to look something like the contents of a coffee percolator. I could hear the man screaming for the woman to let go, and sure enough she did. For a good half minute the air hung silent. Then, in the frontseat of the Cadillac, the woman's shadow bent over low and her arm, or what looked like it, bobbed up and down. When she had finished she closed herself around the wheel again, more slowly and thoroughly than before, and the horn wailed on. I could not see the shadow of the man anymore.

A kid dressed in a tan suit emerged from the crowd. The suit did nothing to hide the dirtiness of his skin. He had a flashlight in his hand and a nametag pinned to his breastpocket. On account of the horn he had to shout at me.

"Those your parents, boy!"

I didn't get the chance to answer him.

"More or less!" my brother yelled. "What you want to know for?"

My brother stood and he told me to stand too. I did.

The kid in the tan suit walked over to my brother. They were the same age and the same size and the same dirty and the same mean.

"I work here!" the kid in the tan suit announced.

"Three cheers for you!" my brother replied.

The kid in the tan suit had red hair. He was ugly.

"You gonna tell them to stop?"

My brother hitched his thumb at the Cadillac.

"They get in fights like this all the time," he said. "I've given up playing referee. You wanna tell 'em to cut it out, go right ahead. It all depends on whether you got the guts to face what comes afterwards!"

The kid in the tan suit's face squinched up nasty.

"Listen!" he shouted. "Them's your folks! And I don't give one inch of a long shit whether they rip each other in half or not, you just tell them to lay off that god-forsaken horn!"

My brother looked at him.

"Tell 'em yourself," he said.

The kid in the tan suit glared at my brother. Then he swallowed some words and turned around and left. As he was walking off I noticed that his pants were crabbing, and when he was a good distance away he yelled, "I'm gonna get my manager and he's gonna call the police!"

"You do that!" my brother hollered. "You go right ahead, tough man!" He nodded at me and we took off then, the noise of the horn falling less and less severe.

About a million people had gathered around the screaming Cadillac, and we had to push our way through them. Practically nobody was watching the movie anymore. I supposed the Cadillac made for a better show.

My brother led me beneath the straddled steel gir-

ders of the Double D screen. We began to climb them like
monkey bars. Occasional tongues of redorange lightning
licked at the topmost tip of the structure, and the steel
beams grew as hot as the coils of a toaster. We were a good
fifty feet in the air.

"What're we doing?" I called to my brother.

He grabbed on to a bar, hung from one hand, and
looked laughing down at me. His eyes were lit fuses.

"We're gonna see Dean close up!" he sang.

He leapt onto a catwalk that bordered the big screen
and did tightrope steps across it. The glare of the screen
painted his skeleton. His ribs were like the bars of a cage.

I paused to catch my breath and looked down at the
world below me. The people were so small I could have
stepped on them.

Above me I heard the cry of my brother and I
climbed up to check on him. The catwalk extended the
length of the screen and was the width and thickness of
two continuous two-by-fours. My brother was doing cart-
wheels on it. I watched him, and after a while, when I
couldn't watch anymore, I turned my head away.

Down on the Double D parking lot the black Cadillac bellowed on. Another million people had gathered and
they stood there dumb as trees as a huge man in striped
overalls cut a pathway through them. He was the manager. He came to the Cadillac and pounded on the door,
but the screaming of the horn did not cease. If anything, it
screamed louder. When the manager realized his banging
wasn't doing any good, he sacrificed manners in favor of
muscle. Gripping the door handle with two ham-sized
fists, he bore down with all his weight in the opposite
direction. The crowd cried aloud as the door snapped

open, then it fell dead silent and took a united step forward.

The manager reached in and drew the body from behind the woman, drew it as calmly as a fisherman might draw the innards from a bellyslit fish. The man in the car had been stabbed several times, and blood covered the lap of his pants as well as the white V-neck of his workshirt. One of his eyes lay closed while the other stared open, and his arms hung behind his head in an attitude of stubborn surrender.

The woman was more difficult to remove. She clung to the wheel and it took no less than four men to remove her.

I looked at my brother. He was doing somersaults beneath James Dean's nose. He caught the guardrail and steadied himself for a moment, then positioned himself upside down and did a perfectly postured walking handstand all the way over to me.

"I'm dizzy," he said. "And I can't seem to breathe."

His skin was the color of technicolor; I could count all his bones.

Redclay swirled in clouds at our feet. We'd left the Double D the same way we came in. I explained to my brother that I wasn't feeling well and he said what I needed was some real food in me, so we headed for the McDonald's where Number One worked.

On the way there it began to rain. It didn't rain hard and it didn't rain long, but I took my shirt off and let it course down my back. I was so tired I wanted to fall down, and in the light of the oncoming traffic I could see the rainwater cutting hard red patterns in the earth.

My brother was unconcerned as to what went on back at the Double D. When he saw the ambulance and police cars surrounding the Cadillac, he made some comment about someone having had a heart attack. He'd completely forgotten that the Cadillac was what we'd snuck in on, that the Cadillac was the car whose stuck horn had interrupted his sleep. He seemed absolutely separated from the events of the evening, and he walked along with his head held high, staring down whatever pedestrians happened to cross his path.

We came to the South Pennymont Overpass and my brother ran skipping up the huge concrete slabs that supported the superhighway. He'd fly up one and dive on his stomach and tumble back down like a moonmad acrobatic. I knew I couldn't keep pace with him, so I sat on the ground crosslegged and watched him. Once he rolled all the way down the cement incline and lay completely still in a puddle of rainwater. When I stood up to see if he was all right, he shot up dripping wet and laughed hysterically. He had a good laugh, like a jackal's. I liked to listen to it.

He finished screwing around and I called to him and he ran to me.

I said his name.

"What?"

"Let's go home now."

He bent down and said, "We can't."

And we didn't. And we were quiet after that.

———

It must have been past ten o'clock as we walked down Asbury Avenue. The porchlights were lit and so were the televisions, and through the front windows the houses shone blue. You could hear the televisions talking and people talking behind them, and sometimes the televisions laughed and the people laughed too, and sometimes the televisions screamed against folks already screaming, and sometimes the televisions fell dead silent and all you could hear was the humming of an air conditioner, or the roar of two cars racing, or a siren, or an airplane, or the breath of your own breathing. And when you heard your own breathing you listened close to it because it wasn't too often that you got to hear it.

Asbury was a sidestreet off Pennymont shaped like a wishbone. It curved into Caritas, which was where the McDonald's was, and behind it in the distance the Pennymont Overpass arched against the sky like a rainbow done in dull acrylic gray. Asbury's folks were every bit as well off as my brother and me, which meant they lived off the same things our family did—tuna fish and minimum wage and rent-to-own television. They weren't as poor as they could've been, but they certainly were poor enough to regret it and boast about it.

All the houses on Asbury looked pretty much the same—small, three-bedroom single stories painted yellow or white or light brown. Lawns for the most part were well kept, and driveways were smirched by patches of motor oil, round slick leakspots covered with sand or clay or deodorized kitty litter. Boys my brother's age worked on cars on blocks on the side of the road, and the cars weren't theirs so much to drive or race as to tune-up and take apart and wash and wax and trade away. It seemed that in the course of ten years a kid could graduate from Hot Wheels and Big Wheels to streetbikes and streetmachines. The best car I'd ever seen was a gold Mustang with black pinstriping that went by too fast for me or anyone to envy. But that car was the exception. It ran so well and often it had to have come from another part of the city altogether, and the driver probably only drove down streets like Asbury to demonstrate the difference between his situation and everybody else's.

At night there seemed to be twice as many kids out and about as there were in the daytime. They hid behind bushes and came whooping like Apaches from around the corners of houses. They played War and Butts Up and Smear the Queer and 500, and in the darkness their eyes were as bottomless as the eyes of cats, their shirtless bodies shiny with sweat and dirt and hosewater. We came across a crowd of kids dancing in a sprinkler beneath the white light of a streetlamp, and I wanted to join them as bad as my brother wanted to join all the guys he'd seen working on their machines. But we weren't invited, and we had things to do, so we shoved our hands down deep into our pockets and walked along quiet and cool and unapproachable.

The storm had reassembled overhead and the clouds clotted black in a coal-colored sky. Lightning fell to the earth seconds before the thunder could warn you, and we passed several chinaberries, black, boughbent, and smoking. My brother had this thing about thunder and lightning and the mysteries of the weather, and at the sight of a smoking tree he'd go to it and take a sample of its charred bark, then roll it between his fingers or scatter some of it in the wind or taste some of it some-

times with the quick tip of his tongue. He was a real
lightning bug, boy. At home, if he happened to awake to
a thunderstorm or some such commotion in the middle
of the night, he'd get out of bed and take off his socks
and go to the kitchen and stand barefooted on the ter-
razzo, waiting for the antennae on our roof to get
struck. "Go to bed immediately afterwards," he swore,
"and you'll dream of heaven all night long." So I tried it
once and got the shit knocked out of me. I woke up
numb the very next morning, facedown on the kitchen
floor. I did dream of heaven, though. The angels had
green eyes and long electric wings. God commanded
lightning from a spinning weathervane.

We came to the curved end of Asbury and were
greeted by a group of children doing a single-file dead
march down the left-hand side of the road. They were
arranged in order of height, from the littlest first to the
tallest last, and a tiny girl with amber hair headed the
congregation. She wore a pink Easter dress and patent-
leather shoes, and she held a shoebox in one hand and a
crucifix with Jesus Christ dying on it in the other. She
was crying. Immediately behind her, a taller boy walked
somberly along. His hands rested on the shoulders of
the little girl, and a burning yellow candle sat collecting
wax and wayward gnats in the pouch of his shirtpocket.
He was crying as well and a candle lit his face pink.
Behind him stood a boy slightly taller and considerably
wider. He had chocolate eyes and a puffy Pillsbury face
and a body shaped like the Liberty Bell, his beige-
colored trousers providing the legendary crack. Every
sixth or seventh step the boy would trip on a rock or
kick himself maybe or stub his bare toe on a gutter
crack, but needless to say he didn't add much to the

straightness of the procession. Who must have been his twin brother stood directly behind him, and despite a similar appearance the boy bore himself with far more dignity. Closing out the procession were three older girls, each roughly the age of my brother. When they saw him they straightened up and smiled available smiles, and the last and prettiest let her shoulder strap slip a little farther from her shoulder than the others' straps had.

"I'll be right back," my brother told me.

He ran to the girl with the available strap and commenced to flirting horribly. She tried to remain straight in line but found herself veering rightward. Her two girlfriends gave her a vicious look, then shot an even meaner one at my brother. Nonetheless, the girl grabbed ahold of my brother's hand and they both came running to me. No less than a minute had gone by.

"This is Lilian," my brother said.

"Hello," I said.

"We're getting married."

I looked at Lilian. She nodded.

"Lilian's daddy is a preacher," my brother continued. "He preaches at the First Baptist Church of Christ Jesus Our Lord Saviour and Most Holy Redeemer."

"On Belcher," Lilian added.

My brother blushed.

"On Belcher."

I looked at them.

"When'd you two decide on this?"

They stared at each other.

"Just now."

I glanced back at the procession as it disappeared around the corner of Asbury.

"What's that all about?" I asked.

My brother prodded Lilian. She blushed so red I couldn't see her eyes. She certainly was something else when she did that.

"It's for my little sister Clara's canary," she said. "Daddy says Gabriel deserves a good Christian burial."

My brother said, "Gabriel's the name of her little sister's canary."

I nodded.

"What you just saw was a funeral procession," Lilian continued. "We're having a vigil with ice cream and cookies too." She smiled. "Wanna come?"

I looked at my brother. He nodded, fast.

"Sure," I said. "Sure, I'll come."

My brother put his arm around Lilian's waist, and the three of us started walking along.

The air was misty and full of night steam. Way far away you could hear the boats coming home to the harbor. They moaned like empty five-gallon jugs will if you blow into them right enough. Up above in the sky a swinging white searchlight swept east and west and back again. Our eyes followed it, and it came to settle on the tile frontporch of Lily's preacher-daddy's house.

The preacher stood on the tile porch doling out cookies to dozens of children, many of whom had not partaken in the procession. Beside them, in the front planter, little Clara knelt in her Easter dress beside a mound of freshly dug earth.

"She's so serious," Lilian said.

The grave was about five feet deep, so the noise of

Gabriel's possible scratchings could not be heard, and the shoebox sat balanced on the lip of the gravesite. Clara was crying harder than ever, and her shoulders rose and fell. Her preacher-daddy stood on the front-porch staring at her sympathetically. He looked like the most exhausted man in the world.

His right elbow leaned tiredly on the sagging handle of a plastic shovel, and he wore the black-and-white attire a preacher is accustomed to wearing at such ceremonies, only the top three buttons of his clerical shirt were unbuttoned, and the upper half of his fly was undone. He had a pale, serious, preacher's face that bore an expression of unbearable weariness, and he was constantly patting the heads of the children, asking them whether they wanted more refreshments. For all his silent misery he seemed a decent host, and when at last the supply of cookies ran out I half-expected him to break off a gingerbread windowsill and divvy that up evenly, but he merely raised his hands a little, cocked his head to one side, and declared in a sad but strong and honest voice, "Sorry, it seems we're all out of cookies."

Out of respect for "the Reverend," as the children called him, and in especial regard for Clara and Clara's Gabriel, who seemed to have been a neighborhood favorite, the children remained despite a lack of cookies. And so, after they had settled down, and after an appropriate late night calm had presented itself, the Reverend let the plastic shovel fall to his side. He approached his daughter Clara and took her in his arms. She was about the size of a basketball.

"Clara," he said, brushing a strand of hair away from the folds of her eyes, "recite for all your friends the prayer your father taught you, recite the prayer that is so fitting and true on this dark August night."

Clara smiled bravely at her daddy. Then she brought her hands across her face and said the prayer that her daddy had taught her.

"Dear Father," Clara said, "I was born with nothing, and will die with nothing. The Lord gives, and the Lord takes away. May His name be praised. Amen."

All the children clapped. I clapped too.

The Reverend lowered the shoebox into the grave. For the sake of formality, he kicked a bit of dirt over it.

"Remember you are dust," he said. "And unto dust you shall return."

There certainly was a lot of dust on the Reverend's shoes. There certainly goddamn was. I turned to my brother.

"Can we start going to church?" I asked.

Our daddy went to church every Sunday. He was the only one in the family who went. He wouldn't talk about it none and he wouldn't take us neither. I had never been dying to go, and ditto for my brother. He barely knew what a church was.

He frowned. "No. No way."

Lilian overheard him. A look of terror fell across her face. She drew my brother's hand from around her waist and took a step back. She looked at him.

"Don't you go to church?"

My brother shook his head and wrinkled his nose. It was like he'd smelled something really bad.

"Ain't you even a Baptist?"

My brother shook his head again.

"Don't you believe in the good news of Our Lord?"

"No," my brother said. "I used to think Christ was a company till a couple years back."

Lilian screamed. Then she fainted.

The Reverend drew a long breath and hurried over to attend to his eldest daughter. He lifted her in his arms and brought her inside. All the children followed.

Many of the kids went directly to the Reverend's refrigerator and proceeded to rifle through it. They shouldn't have done that. The best we could find was a container of Hershey's syrup. I drank it down in one toss and ran outside and Buicked on the rosebushes. I supposed it was my turn.

Back inside the Reverend's house I joined my brother on the outer edge of the circle surrounding Lilian. The preacher sat beside his daughter on a violet davenport, patting her face and hands. "Wake up now, Lilian. Wake up, precious angel."

The children were all very quiet.

One of them asked was she going to die.

The Reverend shook his head dolefully.

"Eventually," he sighed. "Eventually."

My brother touched my shoulder.

"Come on," he said. "Let's get out of here."

We walked through the frontdoor and out across the lawn. It was darker now.

"I thought you were going to marry that girl," I said.

My brother took out his canteen and drank from it.

"Well," he said, "you thought wrong."

He stopped to check his reflection in a pool of rainwater on the hood of a used car. He swept his hair to the side of his forehead and slapped his face repeatedly and lightly.

"I'm still here," he said. "I'm still here."

He pressed the pockets of his eyes with his finger-tips.

I looked at him.

"Of course you are."

He cleared his throat. Gabriel settled suddenly on his shoulder and looked at my brother and flew away.

"You can never be too sure," he said.

He did not put the canteen away—not yet. He took one last long swig from its tipped mouth and broke out into another moonstruck run. He hollered at the heavens like a dog in heat, then the night swallowed his body.

"I'll catch up with you!" I cried, but he did not reply.

I was alone.

I passed the house where the children had danced beneath the spray of the sprinkler. The grass lay flat in spots where they'd tread, and the green blades glistened like stained-glass slivers. A woman sat on the front-porch of the house. She had blue eyes, and I said hello.

"Hello," she said.

I didn't even know who she was.

Caritas looked like a row of candles, and though it was the busiest, most colorful street in the city, it seemed to progress in black-and-white slow motion. The streetlamps and benches and bright orange traffic pylons all felt damp and waxy to the touch, and rain-water crept down narrow gray gutters uttering threats and halfheard curses. For all the arcades, for all the bars and blue-ribbon carlots, the night seemed permanently stilled, and my brother and me strode cautiously through it like the only two people in an unmoving world. Cops in wornblue uniforms leaned like tired statues against the frames of telephone booths, pedestrians stood slackshouldered on trafficdead corners, and a steady stream of cigarette butts dribbled from the yawning mouth of a sewer. I took off my shoes and felt the gutterwater cover my toes. It was as thick and warm as chicken gravy. My brother's face became a balled-up piece of litter. He was disgusted.

"Put your shoes on," he said. "You want to get hookworm?"

"I don't know," I shrugged. "Maybe it's pleasurable."

"Pleasurable?" he snorted. "Pleasurable, my ass." He snatched my shoes away from me and began to undo the laces. He had trouble with a double-knot. "You get hookworm in your foot and that's all she wrote. Pleasurable? No damn sir. Little bugger'll burrow its way through your heel, have your ankle for a snack, gnaw a path clean through your leg, settle down for supper in the tub of your stomach, then make a beeline straight for your ticker. That's his dessert." He bit the double-knot hard with the front of his teeth. "And once that feller gets to your heart," he said, "boy, it's curtains."

I looked at him. He wasn't so much uneducated as misinformed.

"You got it all mixed up," I told him. "It's the tapeworm that eats out your insides, and the heartworm that eats out your heart."

He seemed to consider this from a philosophical distance, then his forehead swelled with the stuff of brilliant answers.

"Naw!" he said. "That ain't it at all, least not half-
ways." He pushed me out from the gutter and made me
sit on the ground and put my shoes on. "A worm that
eats your guts, sure, that's a tapeworm. Everybody
knows that." I struggled with the double-knot he hadn't
undone. "But the worm that eats out your ticker," he
said, jabbing his chest with the stub of his thumb, "that's
what they call that 'ere tickertape worm."

I let my head loll a little, then I looked up.

"Either way," I said, "it don't have anything to do
with no hookworms, which are harmless as far as I'm
concerned."

He huffed. "Little you know."

Just then, several ladies passed us. One of them
said something and looked my brother over and
touched the front of his pants. My brother lost his
breath. When they were gone he said, "Hookworms,
hmph. Turn you into a hooker."

I asked him what a hooker was, but he didn't answer me.

We watched the ladies vanish. One of them got
whistled at and the other three did running tap dances
to open cardoors.

"Why don't them women just walk regular?" I
asked.

"Because," he said, and didn't finish what he was
saying.

At the end of Caritas McDonald's golden arches
rose like the gates of heaven itself. Drivers dimmed
their headlights as they drove beneath them. We stood
far away, but through the glass front of the restaurant
we could see several lines of people. Each customer
craned his head above the head of the customer before

him, and the order board above the counter danced with numbers and food and drink items. It made me hungry just looking at it.

"What're we gonna have?" I asked.

My brother had just finished drinking from his canteen.

"Because he was not dead."

I didn't know what he was talking about. Neither, I supposed, did he.

"Because who was not dead?"

He reached up and brushed something off his shoulder. His head cleared.

"A couple Big Macs," he answered, swallowing and burping twice, "if we're lucky."

We came to rest beneath a revolving clock anchored in the parking lot of a neighborhood bank. The clock stood high in the air and read, "10:14." It was an hour slow. I told my brother what time it really was and he said, "Jesus Christ, that can't be right!" I told him to believe what he wanted to believe, and he grabbed his head in his hands. He said something quietly to himself, then went to the pole and wrapped his arms around it. After a while I told him we had to get going. He spun around with his hands out in front of him and said "okay" about twenty-five times. When he left he walked crooked.

The bank bordered a supermarket which stood directly before the McDonald's where Number One worked. It was closing time at the grocery store and the bagboys were out rounding up buggies. Red-white-and-blue streamers hung between copper-colored parking lot lamppoles, and the streamers made a flapping noise in the late night breeze. Pools of oil-streaked rainwater had collected on the lot, and I could see my own body scatter in a million wavering pieces as I tread unflinching through them. Neither me nor my brother walked around puddles, but whereas I crossed them flatfooted, my brother did a duckwaddle heel-to-toe, toe-to-heel, as if that would make his feet less wet. It didn't. It only took him twice as long to ruin his shoes as much or more.

I crossed a shallow white disk of water and spit backwards into it. When I turned to see how my brother was doing, I found him heels up in the same pool of water. He was staring directly before him, at four bagboys on the far edge of the parking lot. They were smoking cigarettes and getting paid doing it.

"Cocky goodfornothing no-account bastards," my brother said. "Three and a half an hour just to pick their lousy asses." He hated bagboys. "The rest of us folks get to do it for free."

He kicked up some water and it fell all over me.

"I'm going to steal a cart," he said. He didn't need to.

I glanced back over to where the bagboys were and noticed that four more had appeared. They were large.

I looked at my brother.

"Don't do it," I said. "They'll see you."

He looked at me.

"They can see me now."

I shook my head.

"No matter, you shouldn't do it. They'll catch you and hold you down and run your face over with a whole team of buggies."

My brother shoved his hands beneath his armpits.

"I dare them to."

He walked over to a nearby cart corral and

snatched away the biggest buggy he could find. It was every bit as quiet as a train, and all the bagboys swung around.

"Hey!" one hollered. "Where you think you're going with that cart, dudeski?"

My brother paid no mind to him. He brought the cart to me and displayed it as if he'd just bought it. He ran his hand over the metal cage, lifted it up to test the wheels, and unfolded the kiddie seat, which bore a plastic placard. The placard was in red and black and read: "$100 Cash Reward For Information Leading To The Prosecution Of Cart Thieves."

"What's it say?" my brother asked me.

"Just what you think it does," I told him.

The bagboys had begun to mill about. They were all smoking cigarettes for the sole purpose, I imagined, of tossing them fiercely down to the ground.

My brother looked from the cart to me.

"Get in," he said.

I didn't know if I wanted to. I didn't know if the choice was left to me.

"Do I have to?" I asked.

My brother shook his head.

"No. You don't have to."

Another bagboy called out to us: "Hey! You kids! You better bring that groc'ry cart over here! You better bring it back right goddamn now!"

My brother looked from me to the cart.

"Get in," he repeated.

I looked over at the bagboys. They were all gathered in a tight contracting knot. They were still large.

"You sure I don't have to?" I asked. "You say the choice is up to me?"

My brother nodded. His Adam's apple kept nod-
ding its head.

"Get back over here with that groc'ry cart!" a bagboy hollered. "We ain't gonna tell you again! Get it over
here this second or you'll both be dead meat in a damn
quick minute!" He added: "And I mean it!" He looked
like he meant it too. He had arms the size of davenport
cushions and a face like the blistered bottom of a foot.
When my brother didn't answer him he let out a rebel
yell and came charging toward us. The rest of the bagboys followed like bloodhounds.

For the final time my brother looked from me to
the cart and back again.

"Get in," he said.

I looked at him sideways.

"Listen—" I began, but couldn't continue. Beneath my brother's army jacket his chest was beaded
with sweat, and I could see the muscles of his heart swell
and flutter. I imagined he was nervous; he certainly had
a right to be. We could hear the bagboys getting nearer.
The thing was I'd never seen my brother scared before,
and it seemed to reduce him to half his normal size. I
cleared my throat and looked him in the eye. "If I get in
this cart, it'll be because I want to," I said. "Not because
you want me to. I'm tired of you all the time bossing and
ordering me around, sick of you all the time telling me
to do this or that. It ain't brotherly. If I hop into this
buggy, you better realize that it isn't you telling me that
I got to do it this way or I got to do it another, that it isn't
you saying what's right and proper for somebody other
than yourself. You understand?" I said. "Is that the way
it's gonna be if I get into this shopping cart here?"

My brother didn't say a word. His face could've

been uncut stone for all I knew. When the bagboys were so close we could smell the stale Pall Malls on their breath, my brother hoisted me up by the waist and left me ass-high in the shopping cart.

"Goddamn you," he said. "I asked you to get in."

It was like a rollercoaster, sort of, only flat, rainwater cutting like speedboat spray in the spinning path of the buggy's wheels. We tore along, me upside down to a backward passing world, the blood of my body settling swollen in the hollow jug of my head. We flew past lotlamps and lamplights and concrete yellow curbs at a speed twice the sound of anything, one hundred thousand times the speed and sound of everything—the rattle of the wheels tattling clickclickclick and the rumble of the cage rushing thrushthrushthrush and the warwhoops of my brother booking redfaced wingfooted outofbreath and asshauling past the rapid slapping of eight rabid bagboys. Down a quick invisible curb and onto the lot of the McDonald's, cars braking, tires squealing, folks cursing and jabbering at the static-mouth of a paint-peeled pickup window—"Welcome to McDonald's. May I take your order?"—up another, smoother curb across the chirping clay cadence of four and twenty floor tile, passing suddenly and unavoidably through twelve tables of terrified diners, smack into a solid wall of polished glass, me thinking finally and breathlessly as my brother's hands abandoned the steering bar of the runaway cart: "So, this is it. This is the moment not worth waiting for. Close your eyes and take a deep breath and try to remember what comes before nothing." Then, the absolute and all-complete shattering of glass, slivers of which stick upended in me assward—but not only me: caterwauling customers, barking police officers, cornfed rednecks and floor-stricken grandmothers.

I crawled from the womb of the overturned cart and leapt over the counter. My brother was shooting the breeze with Number One, who moonfaced me.

"Glad you could duh-duh-drop in," he said.

Number One had aggie eyes and a bulldog's smile and skin the color of butterscotch syrup. He wore his kinky hair in a sharp high-and-tight and had hands the size of boxing gloves. Next to me he was my brother's best friend, and next to my brother he was mine. He lived with his family at Fort Seltrum Air Force Base, which was less than a mile from where we lived, and me and my brother came to know him by accident.

He'd gone cruising "civvy" neighborhoods on a motocross bike he'd gotten for his twelfth birthday when he saw us doing lawnwork on the sideyard of our house. He decided to show off. He reversed his painter's cap around the crown of his forehead, gritted his teeth and picked up speed, then performed a series of rolling skids, figure eights, and running gutterjumps. Once he'd gotten our attention he stopped where he was, wiped his face with the front of his T-shirt, lifted his bicycle up by the handlebars, and proceeded to pull off a block-long wheelie. When he'd finished he whipped his bicycle right back around, still in wheelie position, and pedaled down the opposite side of the street. He was going along pretty good till he came to a patch of engine grease in the road before our yard. It lifted him off his bike and deposited him backwards on the hard concrete. A line of blood spilled from where his head was opened, and he lay on the pavement staring at the sky. We asked him if he needed any help. He nodded.

"Suh-seventy two two," he said. "Zero two fuh-four."

My brother and I stared at each other. We couldn't make heads or tails out of what he was saying.

"Suh-suh-seventy two two," he said. "Zero two fuh-four."

I scratched my head and studied him. His breathing came in quick shortwinded puffs, like an overloaded engine.

"Suh-suh-suh-seventy two two!" he moaned. "Zuh-zuh-zuh-zero two four!"

I tapped my brother on the shoulder.

"Maybe it's his Social Security number," I said.

My brother considered this and bent down. He asked him if it was.

"No," Number One answered. We didn't know his name was Number One then. "Phuh-phuh-phuh-phone."

My brother slapped his hand against his forehead.

"I get it!" he cried.

He had Number One repeat the phone number so he could memorize it, then he ran inside to dial for help. When he'd gone, Number One looked up at me miserably and let his tongue loll out a little and said, "I ain't never stuttered afore till you guh-guh-guys come along." It made me feel lousy, but it was the truth. His daddy, a shy black man who came to haul him away in the back of a longbed Chevy, verified it.

"What's wrong with you?" he said, looking at him like maybe he was some type of squashed tomato. "What you talking that way for?"

Number One put his arms around his daddy's neck and let himself be lifted into the bed of the truck. "I don't know," he told his daddy, shaking his head confoundedly, eyes rolling back in his head white and milky. "I suppose it was the juh-jolt."

His daddy laid him to rest with a thump. We piled in the back of the longbed too.

"I suppose," his daddy muttered, slamming the door of the truck. "I suppose it was."

Though Number One got his head sewed up, his speech was forever scarred. It didn't keep him from talking none; it was all that boy ever did, you should have heard him. Not a minute went by that he wasn't sputtering on about something, his jaws clapping up and down, head jiggling nervously like a plastic dashboard poodle, lips sucked inward and bulletdrops of spittle spraying outward like some summer sprinkler switched forever on. He was something, all right. It would've been sufficient grounds to drop him as a friend had my brother and I not felt in part responsible for bringing on a condition that was clearly his for life. But Number One was our best friend, and we couldn't've asked for better.

We stood behind the counter at the McDonald's trying hard to look at home and ever-innocent as angels. Number One glanced from the left to the right to make sure no one suspected us. Luckily, the patrons and police officers had pinned the blame on the bagboys, so for the time being we were off scotfree. Number One took both of us by the arm and led us through the kitchen to the backdoor of the restaurant. He paused for a moment on the threshold of the doorway, looking from the kitchen to the world of night outside. Grunting, he threw down the rag he'd been holding in his hand.

"Let's guh-get outta this place," he said. "I'm duh-dead tired of wuh-working here anyway."

We left the McDonald's parking lot a different way than how we'd come in. As we were leaving I saw the bagboy with the face like a foot being shoved into a squad car. My brother saw him too.

"Teach him to mess with me," he said.

Number One looked at my brother and smiled. He patted my brother on the back so hard he coughed.

"Bad man," he said. "Real buh-buh-bad!"

I grinned.

Number One was a little older than my brother, a little taller and wider and wiser too. Though I wouldn't go so far's to stake my life or reputation on it, I might even say that he was the smartest kid I'd ever met, never mind appearances. He walked around dropjawed, like God was stepping on his head, and his size-eleven feet stuck out a good bit farther than the rest of his body. His paws sometimes hung clear down to his knees, depending on the poorness of the day's posture, and oftentimes he farted without announcement nor apology. He talked stupid too. He said things like "warsh and wrench" when he meant to say "wash and rinse," used "ain't" when he meant to say "can't" and "am't" when he couldn't say "ain't," and he was forever using the nonsense word "finna." "I finna be going huh-home," he would tell us at the end of a long day at our house; or, in the middle of a wrestling match, up he'd pop with fists balled fat and a nasty, scraggly look on his face: "I fuh-finna scrap for real!" Once, in an effort to find out why he talked the way he did, I asked him where his family came from. He got a wild look in his eyes, frothed a little at the mouth, and shook me by the shoulders. "Fuh-from the muh-motherfucking muh-moon!" he howled, and laughed for about an hour. He certainly had a mouth on him, for a stutterer and all.

We were heading back down Caritas, in the direction of the air force base. Number One produced a packet of chewing gum from his pocket and held out two fresh sticks.

"Have some Wruh-wruh-Wrigley's?" he said.

We took the gum and unwrapped it and shoved it in our mouths. As I walked along I watched Number One.

He hadn't eaten his piece of chewing gum yet. As a matter of fact, he'd stopped dead in his tracks just to examine it. He held it before his nose with two long pink breakfast-sausage fingers, then his mouth opened up and his tongue dangled out and lapped the gum away. As he worked the stick around in his mouth he began to walk faster, and as the gum settled into a sugary gray pulp he resumed his normal pace, smiling as wide as any split melon. Every time we asked him a question he had to stop chewing the gum in order to think about it. But he wasn't thick, he wasn't thick at all. Or, if he was thick, at least his thickness ran deep.

"Wuh-what'd you guh-guys come and suh-see me for?"

My brother stared at his feet.

"We thought maybe you might wrangle us some burgers."

Number One wagged his head dolefully.

"Tuh-too late for thuh-that," he said. "I done kuh-kuh-quit."

We crossed the intersection at Caritas and found ourselves on Fort Seltrum Road. It was understood by Number One that we were going to spend the night.

"We can play puh-poker," he said, "and tell guh-guh-guh-ghost stories. We can even make crank tuh-tuh-telephone calls!" A look of absolute satisfaction settled on his face. "You two can have muh-my bed, and I can suh-suh-sleep on the cold hard fluh-fluh-fluh . . . on the hard stone fluh-fluh-fluh . . ." He gathered his breath and tried a third time. "I said I can sleep on the cold tuh-terrazzo fluh-fluh-fluh—"

"Floor," we told him.

He smiled.

"You guh-got that right. Floor."

My brother and me'd spent a lot of nights at Number One's house. His folks knew what our daddy could be like because he'd cussed them out for their ways once, and his mother had taken to calling the two of us Romulus and Remus. She was a smart, thin, good-looking lady with pearly white skin, and she read lots of books and fixed a better breakfast than anyone I knew. Number One's daddy was a quiet, secret man. He spent most of his time working on his truck and making homemade beer in the family tool shed. He was a drunk too, but not like our daddy.

"You pop's a puh-puhfessuhpuh . . ." Number One said once. "What do they cuh-call it?"

"A professional," my brother answered.

Whenever Number One realized the impact of observations like this, his soft eyes would cloud up milkier than usual, as if to say, "I ruh-really didn't muh-mean it." But we understood.

As we walked along, Number One proceeded to take off various pieces of his McDonald's uniform. First, he unpinned his nametag. "Get shut of this thuh-thing," he said. Next, he took off his haircap and slapped it down on my head. "Suh-sanitary, they say." Then he unbuttoned his long-sleeve shirt and tossed it in a drainage ditch. "Right where it belongs, tuh-too." The only thing left were his pants, which were his. He tugged on the elastic band and let it snap against his belly. "I'm fuh-fuh-fuh . . ." he struggled. "I'm fuh-fuh-fuh . . . Goddamnit," he said. "I'm fuh—"

"Free," we told him.

He touched his nose and chewed his gum like a horse.

"Buh-bingo," he said.

My brother got a charge out of Number One. Whenever he was around him he couldn't not-grin if his life depended on it. Only thing was, Number One sort of took my brother's breath away. He was too quick and fast and funny, whereas my brother was kind of the hardy-harring straightman. In an effort to shed his sidekick image, my brother kept in store various jokes guaranteed to floor Number One. None of them were any good, but that didn't keep him from telling them.

"Hey, Number One," my brother said, wiping his nose on the sleeve of his army jacket.

"Wuh-what?" Number One asked.

"I got a joke for you."

Number One looked at me. He winked.

"All right. Guh-go ahead."

My brother's face was all loaded smiles.

"What's a Pollock lady put behind her ears to attrac' men?"

Number One thought about it, then conceded.

"You guh-got me," he said. "Wuh-what?"

My brother slapped himself on the side.

"Her heels!" he screamed. "Hardy har har har!"

Number One refused to smile. I didn't get it.

"Like a lead balloon," I told him.

He glared at me.

"You shut up."

A mosquito lit on the tip of my nose and I crushed it with my fingers and licked away the blood. We came to an intersection with a burnt-out traffic light. It had been converted into a four-way Stop, which was buh-better, Number One said, because it didn't guh-get very much traffic, anyway. That reminded him, had he ever tuh-told us the story of the Crazy Red Light Lady? I felt goose pimples roll like dominoes down my spine. Number One told a story damn near better than anyone.

"No," I told him. "No, you haven't. Tell us all about it."

Number One gathered up his store of saliva and fiddled busily with the fingers of his hands. Whenever Number One told a story he made real good use of those boxing gloves of his, sticking them out in front of his belly if he were talking about a pregnant lady, wrapping them tight around his throat when relating the doings of a grisly murder, tapping them quick along the ground if he were playing the part of an old man with a cane, and running them slow down his face in full imitation of a heartbroken kid. Because he couldn't speak right, his stories were five times as long as anybody else's, but that only added to the suspense. Both my brother and I would've stuttered a lifetime in order to spin a tale half as well as he could. Once my brother'd even attempted to imitate Number One's storytelling, complete with stutters and stammers and pulse-ripping pauses of speech. Hearing him, Number One took serious offense. He knocked three teeth clean out of my brother's head. At the Fort Seltrum dentist's office Number One told the outraged doctor: "Sir, a guy can't help it if he stutters his words. He shouldn't be mocked nor made fun of. It ain't right." It was the only time I'd ever heard Number One make it through more than one sentence without flubbing up. Too bad my brother hadn't been awake to hear it.

"The Tale of the Cuh-Crazy Ruh-Red Light Luh-Lady," Number One began, accompanied by a peal of coincidental thunder. "A Suh-Swearin' to Guh-Gawd True Story."

We'd settled down in the middle of the intersection, directly below the burnt-out traffic light. I kept looking to see if any cars were coming, but the streets were washed clean. When Number One spoke the slow-moving world rolled to a dead halt. It was time for everybody to shut up and listen.

I looked at him. He sat with his legs crossed, a mask of dread seriousness fixed across his face, white eyes filled with the black stuff of legends. His voice dropped a notch deeper, and his back set itself straight. I noticed that he wouldn't look at my brother. Instead, he trained his gaze on me. My brother had settled his head in the cushion of my lap and was busy guzzling from his tipped canteen. But Number One's eyes would not leave mine—I was his audience, I had willed this tale.

"Are you ruh-ready?" Number One whispered.

I nodded. It began to rain. The burnt-out traffic light flickered suddenly on, swinging solid red in the slow steady downpour.

"I'm ready," I said.

He began.

"At fuh-four o'clock in the morning, in the muh-middle of a night fuh-full of harmless ruh-rain, it happened.

"I'd just gotten off the late cuh-cleaning shift at McDonald's, had just fuh-finished muh-mopping the floors and shuh-shuh-shining up the old grease puh-pit, and I duh-don't think I need to tell you I was tired as a buh-body could buh-be. I took the same route home thuh-that night that we all took tonight, straight down Cuh-Caritas to Fuh-Fort Seltrum, and it led me to the very spot where we're suh-sitting at now.

"Luh-listen, buh-boy: I was worn down, used up, chewed to buh-bits and spit right out. Thuh-that's how tired I fuh-felt. I thought the next step I'd take was buh-bound to be my last, and I collapsed on the guh-grass on the suh-side of the ruh-road.

"'Is thuh-this what I spend my life wuh-wuh-wuh-working for?' I asked muh-muh-muh ... I asked muh-muh-muh ... uhhh: I said to myself. 'Is this fuh-feeling worth all the work that's been done? The sum tuh-total of wuh-one day's suh-sweat and tuh-tears?' I shook my head for the tuh-tragedy of it all, fuh-felt my

own sorrow creep in ruh-rivers down my chuh-cheeks.
'If this is luh-life in the land of the luh-living, Lord oh
Lord!' I wailed to the heavens. 'Luh-let me uhh-out!' I
was so all-fuh-fire fuh-fed up I tuh-took off my shuh-
shoes and threw them in the duh-ditch and cuh-crawled
like a dog to the center of the intersuh-suh-section. I
luh-laid down my burdened bag o' buh-bones and
stared buh-belly up at the black ass of the night. I wuh-
wanted to die.

   "I suppose I duh-don't have to tuh-tell you this was
before they duh-done put the four-Stop in. Thuh-this
here intersection yuh-yuh-used to be spoke for by thuh-
that there four-sided traffic light. When I finally decided to lay down my buh-burden, I saw way up above
me the old tuh-traffic light shuh-shone red. Thuh-this
was cuh-comforting. It meant no cuh-cars coming
north-to-south could ruh-run me over, and for a while I
was actually huh-hopeful. Then it duh-dawned on me.
One light red muh-means another's set guh-green. Oh,
for a huh-heaven of uh-everlasting yellow! Tuh-tempo-
rary safety from the nuh-north and the suh-south means
guh-guaranteed duh-death from the east and wuh-
west! 'Oh, Lord!' I cried. 'Is there no end to my muh-
misery?' The kuh-kuh-question was no longer whether
I'd get huh-hit, but huh-how, from what duh-duh-rec-
tion would this puh-poor buh-beaten boy at last cuh-
come to pass? From the north, leaving me in the puh-
pavement like a wad of wasted chuh-chaw, or from the
east, leaving my innards to cuh-curl up outta muh-me
like so many worms in a dead muh-man's garden? Boy,
this is the Guh-God's truth: I was at the end of my stick.

   "So I struck upon a plan, a puh-plan to suh-suh-
save my life by my own huh-hands, and buh-better still,

a plan to duh-duh-liver my vuh-very own soul in the event that I got ruh-run over before my phuh-physical salvation.

"I'd give Jesus an ultimuh-matum. If he duh-didn't come an' deliver me from the arms of duh-death by the tuh-time I finished praying—and when I say 'deliver' I mean to impuh-puh-puh-ply live-and-in-person three-D deliverance—if he duh-didn't arrive and lead me by the hand to safety—and buh-by 'arrive' I mean to imply from a guh-golden cloud, with his shuh-shepherd's staff et cetera or muh-maybe just struh-struh-strutting in his fluorescent ruh-robes down the wuh-whiteline Fort Seltrum meridian—if he duh-didn't come to suh-save me from my sadness and exhuh-austion with at least a duh-dash of Huh-Hollywood fuh-flash, I'd let myself suh-sleep the night on the intersection, come hell or travel tuh-trailer.

"Buh-but, as you and your buh-brother wouldn't know, being that you're huh-heathens and cuh-cursed to hellfire anyway, getting to Juh-Jesus is uh-always a roundabout propuh-zuh-zuh-sition. First you guh-gotta go through his mother; she softens him up for the Huh-Holy Spirit. That boy's the salesman, and he puh-primes Jesus for the Big Man. By the tuh-time you've duh-done your appealing through God the Fuh-Fuh-Father, Jesus has gotten such a wuh-working over that he can't huh-help but answer your puh-prayers.

"And as you wuh-wouldn't know, Jesus sometimes answers an honest puh-prayer, 'No.' Which was exactly what huh-happened to me on thuh-that suh-sor'ful August night.

"I cuh-closed my eyes and suh-said the Hail Mary. Listen, buh-boy, and you might learn suh-something:

> *Huh-huh-huh-Hail Mary, full of guh-grace!*
>   *the Luh-Lord is wuh-with you;*
> *Blessed art you amuh-mong wuh-women,*
>   *and buh-blessed is the fruit of your womb,*
>   *Juh-Jesus.*
> *Holy Muh-muh-Mary, muh-muh-muh-mother of*
>   *guh-God,*
>   *puh-pray for us suh-sinners,*
>   *now and at the hour of our duh-duh-duh-death.*
> *Amen.*

And I pictured old buh-blue-eyed honey-haired Muh-Mary walking up behind her Juh-Jesus, tapping that buh-boy on the shoulder, and shuh-showing him my picture.

"'Go deliver this poor lost chuh-child,' she tuh-told him, just like your own muh-mother might ask you to fuh-fetch out the trash. 'Guh-go and duh-duh-liver that buh-boy, his huh-heart is fuh-fit to bust.'

"And then I heard Jesus say something like, 'Luh-leave me be, Muh-Mama. I finna be guh-goin' to buh-bed soon.' And off poor old blue-eyed Virgin Mary went.

"Next I suh-said the Act of Contrition. Duh-don't turn your ears off yuh-yet:

> *O my Guh-God, I am huh-heartily sorry,*
>   *fuh-for having offended yuh-you,*
>   *and I duh-detest of all my suh-sins,*
>   *buh-because of your juh-just punishments;*
> *Buh-but most of all because they offend yuh-you,*
>   *my Guh-God, who are all guh-guh-guh-guh-guh-*
>   *guh-good,*
>   *and deserving of all my luh-love.*

> *I fuh-firmly resolve, with the help of your guh-*
> *grace,*
> *   to suh-sin no more, and to avoid the near occasions*
> *   of suh-sin.*
> *Amen.*

Now that I was contrite in the eyes of the Huh-Holy Spirit, and huh-he'd resolved in his heart that I was a durn guh-good boy, I could suh-see him: in a three-piece suit, Cuh-Cuban suh-see-gar sticking out of his muh-mouth, approaching Juh-juh-Jesus with a port-fuh-folio in his hands.

"'Luh-listen, Jesus,' the Holy Spirit said—though maybe not 'Jesus' so muh-much as 'Hay-zoose'—'huh-here's the guh-goods on this Nuh-Number One indi-vuh-vuh-viddle. Chuh-check him out, I thuh-think you'll luh-like wuh-what you suh-see.'

"But Juh-Jesus wouldn't take no luh-look in the portfolio. 'I huh-heard it from you and I huh-heard it from my muh-mama,' Jesus told the Holy Suh-Spirit. 'And I fuh-finna set stuh-still till I huh-hear it from my duh-daddy.'

"So off went the Spirit and on cuh-came the Fuh-Father, but he wuh-wouldn't make no muh-move till I'd said my puh-prayers. This is what I suh-suh-said; it's called the Our Fuh-Father and it's been nuh-known to suh-save even sinking shuh-ships:

> *Our Fuh-Father, who art in Huh-Heaven,*
> *   huh-hallowed be thy nuh-nuh-name;*
> *   thy kingdom cuh-come;*
> *   thy will be duh-done on earth as it is in Huh-*
> *Heaven.*

> *Guh-give us this day our daily buh-bread;*
> * and forguh-give us our tuh-trespasses as we forgive*
> * thuh-those*
> * who tuh-trespass against us;*
> *And lead us nuh-not into tempuh-tation,*
> * but duh-duh-liver us from Eve-eve-evil.*
> *No amen.*

And Guh-God turned out the luh-lights in heaven, and
cuh-crept to the bedside of his buh-baby boy Jesus, and
Guh-God thought Juh-Jesus looked so puh-peaceful
sluh-sluh-sleeping there that he duh-didn't want to go
and wuh-wake him. But Jesus was awake uh-uh-any-
way—they say he always is—and huh-him and his
daddy commenced to duh-duh-'scussin me. I couldn't
huh-hear what they were suh-saying, buh-but I nuh-
knew it was only a muh-matter of tuh-time.

"So I looked huh-high above me, at the huh-heav-
ens and the tuh-tuh-traffic light. There must've been a
fuh-fuse blown, 'cause all four suh-sides of the luh-light
shone red. For the tuh-time buh-being I knew I was
suh-safe, so I awaited the arrival of Juh-juh-Jesus.

"Some time puh-puh-passed and he huh-hadn't
shuh-shown. I ruh-ruh-ruh-rose up from the ground
and looked to the wuh-west—he wuh-wasn't there. I
tuh-turned my huh-head and luh-looked to the nuh-
north—he wasn't thuh-there. I did an about-fuh-face
and looked to the suh-south, but he wasn't there nuh-
neither. At last I turned my fuh-face to the east and saw
nuh-nothing but a buh-brokendown road. I realized
then that he wuh-wasn't guh-going to shuh-show,
thuh-that the answer to my puh-prayers had buh-been
an undisputed 'Nuh-No!' I fell to the ground and tore at

thuh-thuh-the earth, and when I was fuh-finished I
shuh-shouted to the heavens every buh-bad word I'd
ever huh-heard."

Here, Number One proceeded to list over one
hundred curse words, some in different languages. I'd
never known there could be so many, and I tried my
best to memorize the ones that were good. When he'd
finished, Number One wiped his forehead and spit.

"The duh-devil could tuh-take me for all I cared,
my Juh-juh-Jesus was nowhere to be found. I fuh-fell
alseep.

"When I wuh-woke, huh-heaven seemed no duh-
different from the earth I'd just luh-left. There was a
buh-black-bottomed sky, and a buh-barren stretch of
highway, and a traffic light juh-just like the one I'd
gone asleep to buh-bleeding its ruh-red on an everdead
world. Then I suh-saw the luh-lady.

"She had a wruh-wrinkled buh-body and ruh-red
hair. A guh-green can of paint was suh-slung across her
arm.

"'Leg up?' Thuh-that's what she suh-said to me.
Honest to Guh-God. 'Leg up?'

"Next thing I knew she was stuh-standing on my
shuh-shoulders, her an old lady and everything, a cuh-
can of green puh-paint buh-balanced between her ankles, ruh-resting on my head.

"'Steady,' she tuh-told me. 'Easy duh-does it.'

"She commenced to puh-painting the red lights
green, dropping puh-paint all over my fuh-face in the
puh-process. When she was duh-done she luh-leapt like
a cuh-cat from the puh-perch of my shuh-shoulders,
grabbed me hard with her half-cuh-claw hand, and all
but duh-duh-dragged me to the side of the ruh-road.

Hundreds of cars streamed through the intersection, and I just up and fuh-fainted.

"When I wuh-woke I was on the suh-side of the ruh-road. It was cuh-clear. Huh-heaven wouldn't huh-have me.

"I wuh-walked home juh-just in time for break-fast, and thuh-threw on a nuh-new puh-pair of shoes. Already it was time to go back to guh-goddamn work.

"I headed down Fort Seltrum road to Cuh-Car-itas. The tuh-traffic lights at every intersuh-suh-section I puh-passed were painted guh-green. That was when I knew that I huh-hadn't duh-dreamed about the Ruh-ruh-Red Light Luh-Lady, and I wanted to fuh-find her and thuh-thank her for suh-saving my luh-life. But by the tuh-time the wuh-workday had ended, and wuh-once again nuh-night had fuh-fallen, and muh-men on longnuh-necked suspension luh-ladders had scraped all the guh-green-painted lights back to ruh-red, the wuh-world seemed just as dead, and slow, and ruh-ready to give up. And the Ruh-Red Light Lady was nowhere to be found.

"Thuh-that night, as I walked down Fort Seltrum, I spuh-spotted a police car parked at the intersection where Juh-Jesus nuh-never shuh-showed. A long wuh-wooden ladder lay on the guh-ground, crossed like a stick, and a huh-huge smear of guh-green paint sat spuh-spuh-splattered 'cross the hood of the cuh-cop car. Then I suh-saw that the two puh-policemen were stuh-struggling on the ground with somebody.

"I duh-did not need to guh-guess that it was the Red Light Lady.

"Her forehead was cuh-cut, and buh-blood streamed down her face, and she fuh-fought like a wild-

cat in the arms of the officers. When she caught suh-
sight of me she thrust her arms out in muh-my direction, as if to guh-gather me close to her heart. But one of
the policemen tuh-took out his buh-billy club and ruh-
rapped her over the head. She fuh-fell to her knees
without a sound and they tuh-took her away in the
squad cuh-car."

Number One closed his eyes. It wasn't raining no
more.

"And thuh-thuh-that's the stuh-story of the Cuh-
Crazy Red Light Luh-Lady," he said.

According to the clock on the kitchen wall it was midnight when we walked through the frontdoor of Number One's house, and though I'd rather stare at an open
wound than the face of any clock, there was something
sort of different about this one. It'd been made from the
stump of a giant cypress, had been lacquered and left to
harden till it looked as slick and shiny as a caramel apple, and unlike most clocks it didn't make any noises
that it didn't absolutely have to. I imagined it passed
time better than other clocks too, rushing through that
half hour between hunger and suppertime, letting you
sleep late on Saturdays when it had the power to, and
stopping altogether when you needed a moment away
from everything. I told Number One how much I liked
it, and he said his daddy'd give it to me free for twenty-
five dollars.

Number One told us to keep quiet because his
folks—meaning his mother and daddy and baby sisters
Darcy and Carondelet—were sleeping. This was only
partly true. His daddy was out in the backyard working

on something; we could see his lean humped shadow moving across the curtains of the sliding glass door, and we came upon his mother reading the newspaper in a big chair in the Florida room. She seemed to scan the paper more with her nose than her eyes, and her long dyed honeydew hair hung clear below her rocking-chair shoulders. There was a bottle of cold beer pressed between her legs and she didn't look up when we walked into the room.

Number One cleared his throat.

"Hey Muh-Mama," he said. "I quit my juh-juh-job tonight."

Her tongue touched the tip of her thumb and fore-finger and she turned a page of the newspaper. It did not rustle.

"Then you'll have to get another," she said.

Number One bowed his head.

"Yes, Mama."

He looked at us hard and turned to leave, but the voice of his mother stopped him short.

"Where are Romulus and Remus going to sleep?" she asked. She still had not looked at any of us.

Number One bobbed suddenly on his heels, like he was nervous. He continued to bob up and down as he spoke.

"I don't nuh-nuh-know," he sighed. "I guess my buh-bed. I'll tuh-take the floor as guh-goddamn usual."

I saw the newspaper flutter a little, but Number One's mother still refused to gaze up.

"There will be no profanity in this house. Do you understand?"

Number One poked his tongue out quickly. Had she been looking, she would have seen it.

"Yes, Muh-muh-Mama, I understand."

"And furthermore," his mother continued, "I won't have you sleeping on that cold floor. You'll catch your death. I'll fix you a nice place to sleep on the daven-port, and Romulus and Remus can have the bed in your room." She turned another page of the paper and snapped it to attention; you could tell she was the one in the military and not Number One's daddy. "One more thing. Are those boys going to cause any trouble?"

Number One rolled his eyes and looked at us. My brother was half-asleep on Number One's shoulder and I was having a hard time keeping my eyes open. I was also fighting a terrific yawn; it was rude to yawn in the face of a lady.

"No'm," Number One answered. "I'll try to keep these wild buh-boys out of muh-muh-muh-mischief."

"You'd better," she told him. She broke the spine of the newspaper and let it collapse in her lap. Then she brought her head up, at last, looked me and my brother over good, took a long noisy unladylike swig from her bottle of beer, and belched. But it was all an act—the belching, the paper snapping, the third-degree inter-rogation. On the surface she seemed crabapples clean through, but deep down she was as sweet as any woman could be. The first night my brother and me'd spent beneath the same roof as Number One's mother, we thought for sure she'd creep to our bedside and skin us and scalp us and mount us on her mantelpiece. But we made it through to the light of the morning and came to know her as an all-bluff powderpuff with a grim sense of humor. For instance, when she'd recovered from her own enormous belch and its saucy stench had settled at last in the pouch of our nostrils, she brought her hands behind her head, opened her eyes wide and glassy and green, and said, very seriously, "All right. I suppose they can spend the night. But under one condition."

Number One scowled.

"What's thuh-thuh-that?" he asked.

She curled up into a tiny ball that crushed the newspaper whispering beneath her. She smiled.

"Under the condition that they kiss me goodnight."

I coughed and shook my brother awake; her words stirred like milksnakes in the pit of my bowels.

"What?" he said, noisily. "What?"

"It's Number One's mother," I told him. "She's lost it. She says we got to kiss her goodnight."

As if to ask, "Is this true?" my brother looked at Number One.

Number One nodded.

"Well," he said, sucking in his gut, "I won't do it." He slouched over a bit and jabbed me in the chest with his thumb. "I won't do it, and neither will he!"

There was silence for a moment, then Number One looked from his mother to my brother and closed his eyes tiredly. After a while Number One's mother humphed and shook her head and took up the paper with the broken spine. "I save all my kisses for my husband anyway," she said. And she laughed and laughed and laughed.

Number One blushed wearily because he was embarrassed for her.

"Come on," he said, leading us from the Florida room. "I'll go get the cuh-cuh-cuh-covers."

He returned with the bed things and told us to step aside while he made up the bed for us. We stood there falling asleep upright against the wall, and when he'd finished and told us goodnight and shut the door behind him, we went to bed without even getting under the blankets he'd so carefully tucked and spread and folded. We were so tired we didn't even get undressed. I had my undershirt off and my brother slept in his wet jeans and heavy jacket and bloody pukepocked undershirt, his right hand deep inside his army jacket, holding to the canteen like a little kid clinging to the hollow shell of a dead pet turtle. I could hear him talking to himself and knew it might be some time before he nodded off to sleep.

I recalled how Number One had promised poker games and ghost stories and crank telephone calls, but I didn't mind missing them. I was starved for sleep and felt it come the second my head met the feather pillow. But thirty minutes later my brother was stirring me awake, tugging at my arm and saying my name.

"What?"

"I can't fall to sleep."

I looked at his chin and asked him why not.

"Because," he said. "I can't . . . fall."

He reached into his army jacket and withdrew the canteen. He shook it. It was empty.

"No medicine," he said, rattling like a skeleton. "I'm going. I'm going to go get some."

"Where?"

'I don't know."

He got out of bed, and I rolled out with him.

"It's too late to get any," I told him, cautiously. "Come back to bed and we'll get some in the morning."

He held the canteen in front of my nose and shook it. His eyebrows formed a pitiful "V."

"Need it now. Unh-unh-unh. Can get it at home. It's empty. See?"

"You can't go home now. What if he finds you?"

"I don't care," he said. "Don't care!" He was rattling harder now, like a bone-locomotive, and beneath his breath he repeated: "I'll kill him. I'll kill him. I'll kill him. I'll kill him."

"Shhh." I looked around. "We gotta be quiet. Number One's folks'll hear."

His face was damp with panic and exhaustion. When he opened his mouth two long spittle-strings stretched and snapped.

"I don't care," he repeated. "Listen. I'll kiss her." I knew then he was out of his head. "Do you know what—do you know it? Do you know what he said to me before you barged in?"

I shook my head. He was talking about what had happened at the bait store.

"No," I said. "I sure don't."

He laughed at me then, loud and wicked.

"No! That's right. You don't, goddamn it, do you?"

I saw a light go on in the hallway. My brother saw it too. We were silent and it went back off. My brother's chest heaved up and down. His eyes were the size of two swollen ticks.

I had a thought; I could go get his medicine for him.

"Here," I said. "Let me have—"

I tried to take the canteen, but he grabbed me by the neck and shoved me into a corner.

"Keep your goddamn hands off!"

I looked at him, swallowing.

"I was only trying to —"

"Keep your goddamn hands off."

He had me by the neck still and nothing in his face or eyes moved, except me.

"Listen," I said, my voice barely steady. "I can go and get the medicine for you, if you want. Then you can stay here and sleep while I fetch a fresh bottle. Would you like that? Would that be all right? Listen, now. You just hand me that canteen of yours and I'll—"

It did not take long, and at least it was complete. I'd sensed it coming, but that didn't matter. In one form or another it had happened many times previous. I felt his fist fall in and out of my stomach like a reliable pump, and I'd given up long ago suspecting it meant anything, that he was mad at me for this reason or hurt with me for that. He was just mean; he only needed to hit to hit; and I was the closest thing around to suit his purpose. So I stood there, taking it, held up by the pendulum motion of his arms, and he was like a machine trying to pound something into its previous shape, a shape the machine could only barely remember. As the darkness swelled I remembered the night long ago when my brother and me had crept to the bathroom at the end of our hallway at twelve o'clock midnight. We had candles, both of us, and all the lights were out, and we whispered "Bloody Mary" one hundred times with our backs to the medicine cabinet. If you did this, supposedly, you'd turn to bear witness to the face of the Blessed Virgin lit bloody and weeping in the bathroom mirror. But we were not surprised to see ourselves.

In less than two hours I would find my brother, watching the sky on the roof of our house.

He would be halfdead then.

He couldn't sing worth prunes. His voice sounded like he stored it in a jar of vinegar. A man that size. It was pathetic.

The anthem ended. All I could hear was the clop clop clop of the needle. Nobody took it off. The static sounded like thunder rolling.

I watched him, still. He got in the car and drove away. Well, that was that. I crawled up out of the long grass and felt the blood settle full in my head. I couldn't feel the ground beneath me. I couldn't feel the ground.

I saw the light and I walked to it. It was a guard booth. Mosquitoes hummed around a television and the soldier on duty saluted me seriously. I asked him if he had any.

"No, sir," he said. "Not on duty, sir."

I was younger than him and he called me "sir." I supposed he had to.

"Why you call it medicine, Daddy?"

He empties the golden contents of my thermos.

"Because it makes a dying man feel the world's worth living."

Well, all right.

A jet tore a hole through the roof of the sky and the hole leaked death and darkness and rain. I could reach up. I could patch it up. I walked in the ditch by the Fort Seltrum Road, feeling I could stop speeding cars with my hands. That was why I walked in the ditch.

"What's the best medicine to take for your sickness?"

His face goes cockeyed in the glare of the porchlamp.

"I'd say it depends, my poor boy, on what ails you."

I fell down, rose up, held my head in my hands, felt strapped to both ends of a mile-high seesaw. The world

I *am not his son. He is not my daddy. I am not his brother. She is a whore.*

It doesn't matter what time it is. It can happen day or night. Once it does, you're expected to drop what you're doing and sing along. I dropped what I was doing, all right, but I didn't sing.

In the long grass, on my stomach, I watched them. There were only three. The lady in the station wagon. The private on the moped. The old gray colonel dressed in fatigues. I watched him good.

He slammed the door of his Continental and stood facing the airstrip with his hand across his heart. I counted the wattles beneath his chin, the notches on his straining belt. He had a face like the kissing end of a manatee and I knew he had some hidden in the glove compartment of his car. Men his age always did.

> *Oh, say does that star-spangled banner yay-et*
> *wave,*
> *O'er the land of the free,*
> *And the home of the brave?*

whirled and whirled, folded up and unfurled, and I didn't
move any for a very long while. It was the water in the
ditch that kept me there. It was warm and sweet-smelling
and it soaked clean through.

"Gonna get you squeaky clean!"

*It's the way her voice squeaks on "squeaky" that makes
me laugh.*

"Gonna make a brand new little man out of you!"

*I stand on the counter by the sink in my skivvies. She
strips me and dips me in warm soapy water.*

*"Gonna get you squeaky clean! 'N you say that? 'N you
say 'squeaky'?"*

"Swacky!"

"That's right."

*Daddy comes in and hoists me by the armpits. I hang
stark naked in the light of the kitchen window.*

"Here's your boy, Mama! Mama, here's your boy!"

*She holds me under the water and her hands are soft as
butter.*

Hold me under forever then. Never let me up.

A dirty white pussycat came sniffing at my collar, the
whitest cat I'd ever seen but filthy to the core. Something
slithered in her mouth.

"Mama?"

"What."

*Her hair is a shambles. The car that was there before,
idling, is gone.*

*"Who was that inside with you? When I knocked before,
who'd that car belong to?"*

She makes me a sandwich.

"Ladies from the League of Mercy."

I ask her why she locked the door.

She pauses and tells me, "They had leprosy."

A glass snake in her mouth, that was what it was. She dropped it on my chest and I watched it slither away, a long glittering tinsel-black "S" sidewinding into the darkness.

"Who are you, girl? 'S your name Snow White?"

"She was pure as the driven snow," he sings. "But she drifted."

"Who are you there, girl? Do you have a name at all?"

Her motor said no. "Pert. Pert. Pert. Pert."

I made a fist of my hand and she threw herself against it.

"You like that, don't you there?"

"Pert. Pert," she answered. "Pert."

"Dirty Lil', Dirty Lil', lived on top of a garbage hill! Never washed, never will!" Then he spits. "Dirty Lil'!"

She'd been a housecat, I could tell. But somebody'd dumped her. Now she was nothing but another filthy stray, had by every tom in town, a frayed pink ribbon round her burr-clotted neck. She lived on lizards and trash and bullfrogs. Glass snakes she gave to people.

"Heff!" I said. She shied away. "Get! I gotta go now."

"One day she, said to he, said she to he, 'Will you marry me!' Said he to she, 'never be!'" He spits again. "Dirty Lee!"

I found myself on Caritas.

"Honey?"

He has stopped singing long enough to drain his beer and we sit at the table in the kitchen. She has just finished talking to someone over the phone.

"Yes," she had told the person on the other end. "Yes, yes, yes. No."

Now her hands hide her face like a sheet hides a body. She leans on the table with the weight of her world. The silverware and chipped china shake.

"What's wrong, honey?"

His mouth is full and his jaws work quick and he has not let his fork pause in the middle of asking it.

"Honey, what's wrong? You can tell me."

Below the table her hand falls upon me. She strokes at first, then pats, then squeezes my knee until the skin goes blue. After a while the china stops rattling. She uncovers her face and looks at her plate. She begins to eat.

"Honey," he says. "What is it? You gon' tell us?"

She does not look up.

"It's my mama. She died."

Supper that night is deviled eggs and creamed chicken. Even Daddy licks his plate.

Two hookers leaned on a crossing light and whistled at men in passing trucks. Some men ignored them and some tried hard to and one howled and whistled back and stopped to let the hookers in. They had faces like masks, like solid white Easter eggs dipped in different seltzer-dyes, and their smoky eyes ran with sweat and mascara and the weary tears of the never-sleeping. They talked dirty and laughed loud and dressed in brightly colored rainslickers so they looked like edible Christmas ornaments. All the windows in the shops looked broken, and the jagged glass formed geometric patterns, the glittering work of midnight insects. Beside a hardware store a running faucet spilled bilge-brown water out across the street, and when I went to wash my feet beneath it, the water stopped running. Far off a wino sang a song about John Jacob Jingleheimer Schmidt. I would've asked him for some or maybe even stolen it from him, but you never know what a bum might carry. And when they give you blood in a hospital they give you the blood of bums and whores and junkies. And there's nothing you can do about it—their blood becomes yours.

"Who did this to you?"

Eyes hang like moons in a sky.

"I asked you something, boy. Who did this to you?"

"That's none of your goddamn business."

Eyes go from fullmoons to halfmoons to crescents. Then they are suns.

"All right. All right, then. Maybe I won't patch you up. Maybe I'll just let you take care of yourself."

Throwing down the bottle, then; throwing it down like she had thrown it. Goddamn him. Goddamn him, anyway. He's a doctor, isn't he? Isn't he supposed to?

"Hey," I tell him, thinking what to tell him: "Maybe I won't let you go and patch me up, anyhow. Maybe you won't lay a single finger on me. Some things for hurting, others for healing. I could lie here, couldn't I? Lie here still and stain the floor red. A guy can let you save his life when and if he wants you to, but if he's set his heart on dying, there ain't nothing that can stand in his way. So you're just a go-between. You're just a middle man. You're just the thing they put beneath the leg of a rickety table. So maybe you oughta stop being so nosy about all the business that isn't your concern, and I'll consider letting you save me. But the choice is mine, mister. Mine and not yours." Saying to him, then, all that can be said about it: "You couldn't know. You have to help me. It ain't your choice. You took a oath."

Eyes then, fullmoons once more, round and soft and endlessly deep, two spots of water on a polished mirror.

"It was your daddy, wasn't it?"

Thinking: "*Goddamn you. Goddamn you, anyway.
Goddamn you and the horse you rode in on.*"

At the bar, blue-and-white-striped neon sign draw-
ing in drivers like flies to piss, bellies blocking the entrance
and bellies talking a good game and bellies hanging like
sideways haystacks over green tornfelt pool tables, I saw
the little boy walk in. He wore an undershirt and swimming trunks, and his face seemed a mixture of worry and
curiosity. He crawled beneath the men's legs and stepped
cautiously around glass patches of broken beer bottles, and
when he came to the belly that was owned by his daddy, he
tilted his head and spoke something to it. I couldn't hear
what it was the kid said because I was so far away. I also
had the itching suspicion that I might have been imagining the whole scene anyway, detail by detail, as it came to
pass through the graylit doors of a ramshackle tavern. So
what the kid said went unheard, and his daddy had him
by the ear and out the tavern door with all the bellies
jiggling and shaking in sauced camaraderie. Me, I stood
watching, not doing anything.

I am not his son.
"*Put it down!*"
"I told you to stay in that car!"
"But it was ho-ot!"
"Don't you talk back to me!"

And then he was up again, by the ear, and with his
one free hand the daddy dug about for his car keys in the
pocket of his workpants. When he found them he un-
locked the tailgate of the yellow station wagon that was
his, threw the wailing boy in headfirst, and locked the
tailgate behind him, leaving the key bent and inserted so
the plastic pushlock would remain in a down position. He

grabbed a plank of rotting lumber and wedged it in the station wagon backseat, using it as a sort of partition between the seat and the flatbed so there was no way the boy could get out. His daddy made a sour "I suppose that'll show you" face at him through the steamed-up station wagon window, spit on the ground, and trudged back into the tavern. I watched the bellies ripple in response to the man's return.

"Put it down! Please! Oh God, put it down!"

He looks at the gun in his hand. He looks at her and he looks at me. He is crying below it and maybe I should feed him.

"All right. All right. I'll put her down. All right. All right. I know how to do it."

I went to the station wagon window and stood staring at the boy locked inside. He was crying something at me, but the words were muffled by the thick glass window. So I wrote him a message on the steamwet glass; I wrote something to him that I could write.

"Z-Z-Z-Z-Z."

I am not his brother.

And then his wormwhite finger scribbled from the other side: "O-K."

So Daddy takes the gun and tosses it in the fishing lake. It is late at night and Mama doesn't want us to go but we do anyway. He says he'll take good care of me—"I know how to do it"—and she says she fears for our lives. "If you aren't back in the space of an hour, I'll call the police." By God, she will. And him with that gun in his hand all the way, glinting in the headlights of passing cars, until we pull up at a fishing lake beneath the overpass and walk across the railroad tracks and down the pebble hillside and through the old weed-eaten go-cart lot to some trees that lead to the fishing lake itself which is a good one boy and has some trout in it even if it is smackdab in the middle of the city. And him saying how we'll shoot us some fish, damned if we won't—how we'll wait in the darkness for them to rise for air, and then, when they get a lungful, boy, we'll nail 'em, shoot 'em clean out of the water. And him waving that thing around like it isn't loaded. And the sad curious way he studies me.

"Son?"

"Yes, sir?"

"Go and catch me a squirrel."

"A squirrel? What for, Daddy?"

"Never you mind. Just go and do what your daddy tells you."

I go away and come back because I cannot find a squirrel.

"Son?"

"Yes, sir?"

"Did you catch me a squirrel?"

"No, sir. They were all to sleep, I suppose."

He does not look at me.

"Then go and catch me a whitetail dove."

And I go away and come back because I cannot find a whitetail dove.

"Son?"

"Yes, sir?"

"Did you catch me a dove?"

"No, sir. They were all too fast, I suppose."

He does not look at me.

"Then go and find me a rabbit, boy. The quickest rabbit in the woods you can find. We have to have something," he says, "to shoot."

And I go away and come back because I cannot find a single quick rabbit.

"Son?"

"Yes, sir?"

"Did you catch me a rabbit?"

"No, sir, no. They were all too slow. You wanted one quick, but I caught every one."

And he looks at me then and pulls the trigger back.

"Well. How fast can you go? How fast can you run?"

And I fall at his feet, tearing the earth.

"Not fast enough, Daddy! Not fast enough!"

So he takes the black metal thing and tosses it in the fishing lake.

"I know how to do it," he says, finally.

He gathers me up and he carries me home.

At the corner of Caritas and Pennymont he sat, legs crossed Indian style, head thrown back in drunken song.

John, Ja-cob, Jin-gle-hei-mer Schmidt,
That's my-name-too!
When-ev-er I come out,
Peo-ple al-ways shout—
John, Ja-cob, Jin-gle-hei-mer Schmidt!
Da da da da da da da!

He wore a red-striped tanktop and his muscleless arms and shoulders drooped and sagged inside of it. His gray slacks were caked in filth and his naked yellow feet dangled in the gutterwater. When he sang his chest collapsed in and out like an accordion draped in flesh, and a high-pitched whistling noise rushed from the toothless hollow of his mouth. He held a bottle of MD 20/20 in his right hand, and a Mickey Mouse watch without a watchband in his left.

"What time is it!" he screamed, cocking a crazy eye and slapping his stomach. "What time is it, children? Oh, yes! Oh, yes!"

I tried to ignore him, but he called to me.

"You there! Come on over! What's your name? You there!"

I figured maybe I could talk with him and swindle him out of some of his Mad Dog. That would be enough to do me and then I wouldn't have to go home and risk facing him. I hoped that the wino was a decent drunk too and didn't have anything lethal or contagious about him. I hoped he was clean some.

I was next to him.

"What's your name, son?"

He asked it like someone might ask you whether you had a lit bomb behind your back.

"What's your name, son? Everybody's got a name, even the poor."

I started to tell him and he interrupted me.

"Hush! Hush! Names aren't important, that's one thing life's taught me. Only reason you learn a name is so you can remember to forget it. Yes Jesus sir. I'll remember you, boy, but the hell if you expect me to remember your name. Even the poor, you know."

I glanced at his bottle.

"Hey, man. Gimme a swig?"

He grinned and showed me his labrador gums.

"Nothing doin', partner. First you gotta ask me what *my* name is."

The rain commenced to pouring down heavy.

"All right," I said. "What's your name?"

He looked at me goofy and cocked his ear.

"What's that?" he shouted above the rain. "Speak up!"

I looked at him.

"What's your name?" I repeated. "I asked you what your lousy name is!"

Again, he played like he was stonedeaf and stump-mute. The hand wearing the watch flew up to his ear.

"How's that?" he said. "Reit'rate yourself! This old boy's got wax in 'em!"

I planted my fist on his shoulder and leaned over and bellowed in his greasywhite ear: "Your name, I asked you! What's your goddamn name!"

He jumped to his feet, let the Mad Dog break on the ground, and proceeded to perform a drunken side-walk jig. "Brother!" he cried, slapping my arm—

John, Ja-cob, Jin-gle-hei-mer Schmidt,
That's my-name-too!
When-ev-er I come out,
Peo-ple al-ways shout—
John, Ja-cob, Jin-gle-hei-mer Schmidt
Da da da da da da da!

I left him there, dancing naked-footed in the broken glass and pouring down rain.

"Later, John Jacob!" he called after me. "Every-body's got one! Even the poor!"

His nose presses against the glass door. Clouds uncurl around an opened mouth. He is watching her, but she doesn't know. I am watching him, but he doesn't know. It is because his eyes are my eyes and his hair my hair that I am watching him who is watching her and how, in turn, we are all watching each other. It is because he is not my brother and she is a whore that I see the things I see and do the things I do. And through the glass front of the grocery store they both watch each other and pretend not to. Through the glass which is as clean and shiny as the inside of a coquina shell I can see her through him, her who is a whore. I can see she has something to tell me.

It sat unlit at the deadend of our block. There were fist-sized holes in the porchscreen, and the swinging door hung unhinged and groaning. Paint flaked like fishscales from wooden slats on the side of the house, and clumps of dark green sandspur weeds clustered in the sideyard like clenched fists. I knew, going in, I'd have to be quiet. He wasn't exactly dying to see me.

She holds him in her arms like a loaf of warm bread. His mouth opens and closes and his hidden eyes try to. I run my hand over the bowl of his head, which is as soft as a bruised peach.

"What's his name?"

They tell me.

"Where we going?"

"To church."

So we dress, and pile in the station wagon, and they hand him to me, to hold and watch over.

"What's 'church'?"

He looks at me in the rearview mirror.

"Hush. Mind your brother."

His back is turned so I can't smell his breath. If it weren't I could smell it and it would smell like the bottom of a bottle. Maybe a bottle of medicine, even.

"What'd you say his name is?"

She turns down the radio and tells me again.

I think about it.

"Oh," I say. "It's a pretty name."

And I hold him struggling in my arms. He is my brother. But now he is not. Was, is not, isn't: how I miss him.

"Come on."

I unlatched the gate leading to the backyard, stepped through, and mounted the stairs to the backporch. The ceiling fan whirled in the glow of a lightbulb, and two spiderwebs hung in either corner of the room, clotted with the bodies of trapped and bandaged insects. A white light bled through the lip of the backdoor, and I could hear the television talking inside. That meant either one of two things: he'd fallen asleep on the davenport in front of the TV, or he'd gone back to bed and had forgotten to turn it off. If he were asleep on the davenport, I would have to get past him. I would have to walk through the living room, up a step to the kitchen, and then to the medicine cabinet. It had a key and a lock, but it was always open. It was always open and it was always stocked.

"Every man has a hobby," he said, once.

In we walk, quiet as a quick piss and slick as Sunday spittle, and all the people in ragged clothes stand in long lines outside dark wooden boxes. They look wasted and wounded and worse than forlorn. They look dead before their time.

I ask my daddy what's going on.

"Confession," he tells me. "They're confessin'. They go in dirty and they come out clean."

"An' you do that?"

He nods his head.

"I most certainly do."

"Sir?"

No one answered.

I walked in.

Beside the glittering basin, it happens. Daddy makes a cup of his hands and dips it down in the water. Mama takes him from me and holds him while they let the water trickle. Then he cries and fights and they pronounce his name together. All the ragged people stare. I ask them have they ever poured water over me. I ask my mother and father, both.

"No," they say. And it is not a lie.

The sports page lay scattered across the floor of the living room and a plate of red beans and rice sat atop the Jai Alai results. A couple Christmases previous they bought me a busted cesta. I didn't really know what to do with it and had a hard time getting it to stay strapped to my forearm, but eventually I got some use out of it. With a pocketful of shagballs I'd stolen from a driving range, I'd take the cesta down to the K-Mart and practice my shots against the department store wall. Sometimes I got the ball going pretty good, but I misjudged a bounce once and it chipped my two front teeth. My mama and daddy got a big charge out of that. They said maybe they should have given me my two front teeth for Christmas instead of some old Jai Alai cesta. They said it was a question of hindsight over foresight and laughed themselves into a double hernia. I wound up selling the cesta for the crippled remains of a bumper pool table, and they never knew about it.

I peered around the corner into the kitchen. He wasn't there, either. Empty beer cans sat crushed on the countertop, and a heavy black cast-iron skillet lay soaking in the sink. He had a portable radio he carried with him at all times to help him fight his loneliness, and he'd left it running on the kitchen counter. I went to it and picked it up and cradled it in my hand. It buzzed and was warm and I fiddled with the stations. I came upon a madwoman.

She was unhappy, she said. She was alone. Her husband
had departed and her children were married and she
didn't have the qualifications to land a part-time job. She
said she felt worthless and couldn't sleep nights and was
this close to losing her mind. If something didn't change
somehow soon, she'd hurt herself, she swore she would. I
didn't know what the hell she was doing on the radio, a
woman like that, taking everybody in the awful world
down with her, but then I heard the comforting voice of
the talk show doctor she'd called for consolation. First the
doctor told her to settle down. "You're not about to lose
your mind," he said. "You're not about to hurt yourself."
He asked her if she had a pencil and paper. "Yes," she told
him, "I've got my writing things somewheres about the
house." But wouldn't you know it? She was just too nervous and distraught to go about finding them right then
and there. It didn't faze the doctor any. He asked her if she
had an adequate memory and she said yes, her memory
was like an elephant's. The talk show doctor got some
mileage out of that; he laughed for the better part of an
hour, like he'd never heard anything funnier in all his born
days. Then he got real sudden serious again and asked
the lady if she had a library card. "Why, 'course I do," the
lady told him, but her voice kind of trembled when she
said it, like she might have been fibbing to him. If you
were to ask me, she sounded like she'd never even read the
phone book, like she couldn't even read her own pitiful
name were some poor sucker forced to scribble it out
before her. Truthfully, she sounded like I sound when
somebody asks me can I read, which I can't, or write,
which I can't do none of neither. But the woman just
wagged on, saying yes, she had a library card, had had one

for years, and it was so yellow from checking out books you'd think that she'd used it to spread mustard. Of course this last remark had the talk show doctor on the goddamn floor, you could just see him choking all over himself, but after he'd recovered he told the lady to pay careful attention. He was going to rattle off a list of highly recommended books. "Are you ready, dear?" he asked her. "Yes, sir," she said. "I'm ready as I'll ever be." He proceeded to run through the titles of ten or fifteen books whose names I could barely figure out, let alone remember, about stuff I'd never in all my life heard of—stress management and the empty nest sin-dome and post man-o'-war depression. Then he asked her if she was still there and she let out a dogwhipped peep of a "yes" and he said "good" and if she had the time she might also want to check out the biographies of Catherine the Great and Queen Victoria and Eleanor Roosevelt and other significant women, but before the doctor could finish listing those she told him about a picture book of the Blessed Virgin Mary she had hidden in the bottom drawer of the dresser in her empty nursery, and would it be all right if she just looked through that every night before she went to bed? That was when the background music welled up and a young guy with a husky voice came on and talked about his girlfriend's bluejeans, which was followed by a message sponsored by the Episcopal Church and a brief advertisement for inexpensive abortions. I turned off the portable radio and stared down the unlit corridor that led to my daddy's bedroom. There was no light beneath the doorway, which meant he was asleep.

"He's just resting's-all. You run on home now and we'll take care of him for you."

"If he's resting, I can wake him up. If he's sleeping, I can wake him up and take him home on my own. I can drive the truck now and I wouldn't be beholding to you."

They look at each other and their leathered cheeks color.

"It's not a question of being beholdin' to anyone, boy," says a man tending bar in portly bib overalls. *"We just don't want you to wake him up's-all. He looks so pretty, you know, sleeping there."*

A man in the back of the tavern laughs and hoists his beer.

"Yeah! He needs his beauty sleep!"

None of the other men find this funny and I stare at the man with the beer in the back and he stares right straight back through me. He starts to move, closes in, like an angry dog circling something.

"You watch the way you look at me, boy. I'd sooner hurt you than look at you, and I mean it. You gon' wind up jus' like your daddy—dead drunk on a piss-wet floor, dreamin' a heaven and the whore that done left him. So you just watch the way you look at me. I'd sooner hurt you."

They lead me out by the arm then, the large sad man in the bib overalls swearing that he'll look after him, that he'll get him home safe. I get in the truck and take it to the all-night lot on Cranston. They give me $750. I burn $500 with a match and toss the other $250, bill by bill, into the bay. When she finds out she locks me in my room for a week and brings me meals she wouldn't otherwise cook. Daddy brings some in flasks and bottles and small paper cups when she isn't looking. He is not upset about the truck. "It took a fair amount of courage," he says.

No light at the lip of the door. No sound of unsleeping from inside. And the air was suffused with a sweet hot

smell, like the air in the LB&T, like the smell of anything
bleeding fresh.

"*You leave him the hell alone! Keep your goddamn
hands off him!*"

"*You can't talk that way to me. I've got this piece of
paper.*"

"*I don't care what you got! I'll talk to you any way I
damn well please!*"

"*No you won't, son*"—*looking at me*—"*your mama
won't hear of it.*"

*I rush him. His fist falls across my face two times quick. I
am bleeding, but barely.*

"*Goddamn you! Goddamn you!*"

"*You can't talk that way to me.*"

"*Goddamn you!*"

"*Why, I've got this piece of pa*—"

*I rush again and meet the floor. It is hard and black and I
am beside my father. The shape of the man looms weaving
above us, a piece of white paper hanging from his hand.*

"*Read it.*"

"*He can't.*"

It is my daddy, rising.

"*Read it, son.*"

"*I said he can't, you son of a bitch! He can't read 'cause
he's illit*—"

*And the man doesn't even look at him. The fist with the
piece of paper in it lands hard and fast across his face. The blood
flows from his lip and draws a crescent on the floor. There is
blood on the piece of paper and the man looks at it as if he's
going to cry.*

"*Take it like a man, Bohannon,*" *one of them says.* "*It'll
hold up in court, all right.*"

But he only shakes his head and holds the paper before him. It seems to bleed of its own accord in the glare of the overhead light. Some of the drops fall to the floor. They fall slowly. The man is rocking on the balls of his feet and moaning. His face is wrung with sweat and exhaustion.

"I wanted him to read it for himself. I wanted him to read it and know. But now it's tainted—look at it bleed. It's tainted with blood and ain't no one ought to read it."

He leaves.

And I was not his son. And he was not my father. And I was not his brother. And she was but a whore.

And what I'd always been before became now somehow different, and those I'd always known and loved were each no longer there. It was as if a hand had taken my name and erased it, and there in the place where the name had stood was a space all black and empty. And I thought, "So this is how it feels. So this is what it's like." And I remembered how it used to be, a while back, when it wasn't. Life was a filled-up feeling then, a thing you carried around in your arms like a ten-gallon jug of icewater. But one day my mother came and took the jug and drank—and it was half-full. Then another day my daddy came and tipped the jug to his mouth—and it was fully empty. And I spent what seemed the better part of my waking moments searching for someone to fill the jug up, but nobody did; it was permanently hollow. So I dreamed of the days when she'd bathe me in the sink, and I'd long for the nights when we'd sneak out to fish, and at last when he came I tried to carry his jug for him, to keep them from drinking any or him from spilling his share, but it was no use. The world came along with a hammer on its arm, and both of us fell shattered on a piss-wet floor.

"Daddy."

"Daddy?"

"Daddy," I said.

I opened the bedroom door and waited, but there came nothing—nothing save the sweet stench of poor wine spilled. He lay in bed, on his back, wrapped in a purple robe, and his head and arms dangled over the lip of the bed where the darkness reached. All I could see, mostly, were his parched feet. They were as yellow and broken as a turtle's underbelly, and his stomach hung frozen in midbreath like the swollen body of a drowned animal. He was dead drunk, I could tell. Nothing I might say could wake him now.

I studied him.

"Daddy. Wake up."

He didn't respond.

"Wake up, Daddy. Come on, get up."

Carefully, I sat on the edge of the bed, at his feet.

"Pssst! Daddy! It's me, you son of a bitch. Wake up and look at me. My face, my eyes. I'm drunk and bleeding and out of my head. That's proof enough that I'm yours forever."

Still, no response came.

"Possum!" I swore. I prodded his foot, and through his calluses and plantar's warts I was sure he couldn't feel a thing, so I got up and went to what used to be my mother's vanity. I found a pin cushion in the bottom drawer and I took it and went back to my daddy and sat beside his feet. Then I drew a pin from the cushion and stuck it in him.

I imagined I heard a moan, but it was only the wind in the palms.

I cursed him.

"Wake up, raggedy doll! Get on up, goddamn it."

I drew another, longer needle and pierced the fleshy part of his other foot. He didn't even bleed none.

"Come on, you sad sorry son of a bitch. Wake up, now. Come on."

But he wouldn't stir, he wouldn't even flinch, and the needle sagged inside his flesh almost as if it were being drawn down deeper. That was when I realized that there was nothing I couldn't do to him, that I could've put a kitchen knife through his side without him so much as smacking his lips.

Out of curiosity, I took the longest needle I could find and stuck it in my own hand. Because I could feel it hurt I knew I needed some, and I ran from the bedroom, down the hallway, to the kitchen. That was when I saw that the medicine chest had been opened.

It was like somebody had been there and left, like a ghost or something had ransacked through it. The terrycloth towel my daddy'd put there to hide the stock from plain sight had been ripped and it hung in two halves, and there was no medicine to be found in the cabinet. It was obvious that my daddy'd drunk every drop dry, and I was sure if I went out to the backyard, I'd find a stack of empty bottles. But I didn't have the time to look, so I shut the swinging doors of the cabinet and walked back down the darklit corridor.

Walking, I had the strangest feeling. It was that the house and everything in it had died. I didn't know why I felt the way I did; it must've been a couple things that set it off. There was the quiet without the TV, and the quiet without the radio, the quiet of the night, and the quiet of nobody talking. There was also the great beating heart of the air conditioner, which was still, and the silence of the refrigerator, which wasn't working right no more. What I noticed most was the lamp on the frontporch. I didn't know if it had blown a fuse or was just short a lightbulb, but it didn't cast nothing but darkness. It made me feel sort of blue looking at it through the window near the pantry, on account of that was the light that kept the night off me when I was little, that was the light that had warded off burglars and welcomed-in company and thrown checkerboards of light across my chest and shoulders and face and arms when I slept in the bedroom that bordered it. But now the lamp was gone and had that look of being unlit forever. The front of our house faced the street blind.

I was convinced the house had died when I heard the noise coming from the unopened doors of the hallway pantry. It was a sound like bones rubbing slowly together, and as I opened the pantry doors I imagined I might see two skeleton joints coming together to spark a furnace. But what I saw was worse.

There, pouring out of cereal boxes and skittering across nonperishables, were more roaches than I'd ever seen gathered in one place in my entire life. They were quick and fat and covered with what looked like powdered sugar, and with their crooked legs and dark eyes they resembled pieces of moving chocolate. Usually, whenever I'd come across a couple roaches nosing through the cupboards, they'd run like hell to get away from me, but not these fellers. They swarmed in and out of bags of corn starch, stood double-decked on top of one another sniffing at unopened jelly-jar lids, and burrowed their way as deep as they could through paper sacks of packaged sugar. It was like they were organized, and I stood there watching. The noise they made was crisp and brittle, like a cat working its teeth around a yardbird, and I supposed the noise came from the way the bugs were packed in so tight together. Now and then a pair of roaches would light from the shelf and settle on my arm, and though at first only a few were brave enough to leave the sugar shelf, when they realized I was friendly the rest came to call. Some found their way up my shirt, others gamboled about in the forest of my hair, and a few dozen came to form a pointy crown around my forehead. After a while I grew sort of heady with the unbelief of it all. I tried to brush the roaches off with my hand, but it wouldn't do no good. It was like the critters were made out of air, and my hand brushed right through them. I decided I couldn't beat them, that there were just too many, and I fell to the floor with my arms at my sides while the roaches covered me over like a pile of dirty laundry. I imagined that when I rose up I might be nothing but a stack of bones, all picked clean by the bugs on top of me, but when I finally stood myself back up I saw that the roaches had gone. I even checked the pantry and they weren't there either. What's more, the bags of corn starch and canned goods and pack-ages of sugar looked like they'd never been touched. That was when I realized I had imagined it all, and I reached for my daddy's fishing knife on the topmost shelf, because I didn't know what I might imagine next.

"*Me and him are going for a ride in the country. You wanna come?*"

"*No. You two go ahead. What time will you be back?*"

"*Oh, I don't know. Six, maybe.*"

"*Before supper?*"

"*Why, yes. I suppose we can be back before then.*"

"All right," she says, going over to kiss him. "Goodbye."
"Goodbye."

I walked in with the knife in my hand and the room was even darker than before. It was even sweeter smelling too. I wondered if the sweetness came from the picture of her on the bedside table which he sprayed with cologne and kissed each night before he went to bed, drunk. I saw him do it once when he was lit and it was almost as embarrassing as the time I found her halfnaked.

"What're you—"

"Quiet! Shut that door! You want the neighbors to see?"

Her body is pale and full and she does not rush to dress. She walks past me slowly and I can smell her, the way she smells. My face is a rush of blood as I watch her walk to the long mirror with the man's shirt and the worn money held up in front of her. From behind her, I can see her, from below her, I can see her, in the mirror, that sweet womansmell and what I never knew nor saw. She brushes past me again slowly, flushing in the long mirror.

"Mama—"

"Hush! I'll get decent soon. I just can't seem to find my silk slip nowheres."

Turning, her hips, her bottom, facing me now, turning away, legs bending, curving up, hard on what I was hardly meant to—

"Ha ha ha!" A hungry crow, laughing. "Look at you! Stop your gawking there. Ain't you never seed a naked woman before?"

"No, Mama, no"—swallowing, breathless—"I haven't ever seen a—"

"Shhh!"

She rushes to me and holds the man's shirt over my mouth. Her body is beside my body, and I can feel the warmness of her nearness. Her chest rises and falls. Outside, slowly, a car drives by. I can hear it stop, reverse, and idle before our driveway. "Listen," Mama whispers. "I'm gonna go see who that is and I want you to stand still. You've seen enough of me this morning without having to gawk no more." But when she leaves I turn around and watch her in the sunlight of the kitchen window, her skin the type a hand would move to, her body barely trembling. She is waving at the person in the car. His motor is not our daddy's. She is waving to the person in the automobile. She is waving him away.

I turned my head from her picture to the shape of my daddy on the rollaway bed. He was dressed like a king in his lavender bathrobe, his royal belly puffed high like a rotting pumpkin. I took the fishing knife and laid it across him. It wouldn't be very difficult. He was so gone he wouldn't feel anything anyway. All I'd have to do would be to point the blade down and throw the weight of my body on top of it. Then he wouldn't have to face it no more.

With one hand, I tightened my grip on the knife. With the other, I felt the place where he'd hit me just hours before. I wondered why he struck me. He said it was because I wasn't his goddamn son, but we both knew it was something more than that. I'd tried to save his life and he'd hit me. He was this close to choking on his own vomit and puke and I had helped him and he'd hit me. He looked at me once and what I had done and the man said I had saved him and he'd hauled off and hit me. I thought about it and thought about it, but couldn't get much of anywhere. Maybe he had wanted to save himself. Maybe he had wanted one of his friends to help him. Maybe he was ashamed that his own son had saved him. Maybe he had not wanted to be saved at all.

I took the knife and stood over my daddy. Outside, the wind had turned to rain and the palm leaves sang like the souls of the dead. From across the yard came the noise of a piano, and from across the city the song of a siren. I pointed the blade downward and grabbed the handle tight. I was chattering and trembling, but I managed to steady myself. When I fell, and the wetness sprung up from under me, I thought to myself how easy it was, how it didn't take much effort at all. You just grab on to the thing, hold it steady, and hurt it so bad it can't go on no more. So I wasn't even killing him. I was witnessing a death.

I finished and went to the bathroom and washed my hands, then I came back to the rollaway bed and sat beside him. It was more sweet-smelling now, and the rain had died, and the bed was covered with my daddy's wetness.

"It don't take much work to make something dead."

That was what I told him as I sat right there beside him.

"It don't take much work at all."

I remembered how I still had the knife in my hand, and how warm it felt, and how I wasn't even crying. There really wasn't any reason to cry, at least not then, at least not yet.

"Not much work at all."

Once, a long time past, my daddy took me for a ride in the country. We listened to rock 'n' roll on the radio and stopped to buy strawberries from a roadside vendor. My daddy didn't have any medicine the whole time I was with him, and when we weren't listening to the songs on the radio, he would talk to me. It wasn't much, really. Just talk. But it was something, all right. It was goddamn everything.

I am not his he is not my she is am is I—

Because *I am not his* killed him, because I had only witnessed a death, I rose from the bed to stare at the face which wasn't even there, at the shotgun which lay across his shoulder, at the fantail of blood and smoke on the far bedroom wall.

It was a bad hurt.

I stood before the full-length mirror in the bathroom at Number One's house. Everybody was asleep. It was barely past two o'clock and I could hear them snoring. I busied myself inspecting the places where he'd hit me. There were two patches on my sides, and a rising purple splotch on my stomach. My lower lip was torn a little and dribbled blood, but it wasn't as bad as it felt. I knew there weren't any broken ribs or anything.

After a while I turned my face from its reflection and shut out the light in the bathroom. I sat down on the toilet seat. I must have been crying louder than I thought because I heard footsteps coming down the corridor. Number One knocked at the door, briefly.

"I'm all right," I told him. "Go back to bed."

"Nuh-uh," he answered, whispering. "You open this duh-door right now or I'll wuh-wake my muh-muh-mama."

I waited awhile before I answered him, staring into my hands.

"You wouldn't do that."

"No," Number One answered. "I wuh-wouldn't. Yuh-usually. But in your cuh-case I'll muh-make an exception."

I sat in the darkness for some time wondering whether I should call his bluff, but before I had a chance to open the door myself, which I would have done, eventually, I found that he'd picked the lock with one of his mother's emery boards. He stood in the shadows like a slumped-over ghost and ran his hand over his whole face. He pooted and said, "What in Guh-guh-God's name has guh-guh-gotten into you, little puh-puh-pecker? What're you doing luh-locking yourself in other folk's tuh-toilets thuh-this hour of the nuh-nuh-night?"

I didn't say a word. He stepped into the bathroom, locked the door behind him, and turned on the over-head. When he saw the shape I was in, he just said, "Suh-suh-ummm-bitch," over and over. After he'd fin-ished admiring my battle scars, he left the bathroom and went to the kitchen and brought back a bottle of alcohol and a washcloth. "Luh-lemme see your luh-luh-lip," Number One told me.

"You can see it," I said to him.

He scratched his neck and grinned.

"All right," he said. He handed me the alcohol and the washcloth. "Clean yoursuh-suh-self up, then. I ain't guh-gonna muh-mother you."

I took care of my cuts and bruises and handed him the alcohol. He took the washcloth and ran it under the sink and gave it back to me. I placed it over my eye; a real shiner was welling up.

Number One said, "Your buh-brother treats you buh-bad. You nuh-know that?"

He sat in his long underwear on the lip of the bathtub staring at the blisters and mosquito bites on his feet.

"If yuh-you were my buh-brother," he went on, "I wouldn't tuh-treat you like that."

I took the washcloth off my eye, squeezed it dry into the sink.

"I'd tuh-take care of you, and guh-give you things, and tuh-teach you to fuh-fight so guh-guh-goddamn good I'd be afraid to lay a hand on you. Listen." He looked at me, lifted his eyes from his awful feet and looked at me. "You ain't like your buh-brother. You're sharp, and you got suh-suh-suh-sense. How cuh-cuh-cuh . . . how cuh-cuh-can you let him tuh-tuh-treat you like he duh-does?"

I looked at him.

"I ain't got no choice."

He tried to keep his voice down.

"You shuh-shore as hell do!"

"No, I ain't."

"Guh-Goddamn it!"

"I ain't got no choices. Not about him nor nothing."

"You little puh-puh-pecker!"

We must have been being too loud; from the direction of Number One's parents' room there came a yell. It wasn't "Shut up!" or "Go to bed!" or anything, really, just a yell. Number One took his hard eyes off me and shoved me out of the bathroom and shut out the light and took me to the kitchen, where we could talk. He tried to make me sit down at the supper table—to talk some "suh-suh-sense" into my head—but I wouldn't hear none of it.

"You suh-suh-suh-sit down now. You luh-listen to me."

"I can't. I got to go."

"Go? Guh-Goddamn it! Where tuh-to? You ain't guh-got nowhere to guh-go tuh-to!"

"I do too."

I started to leave, but he grabbed my arm.

"Let me go, now."

"You ain't got no suh-sense."

I turned on him.

"You just said I had!" I told him. "You said I was sharp! You said I was sharp and had sense not two seconds ago!"

"Wuh-well," he stammered, shrugging his shoulders. "You shuh-shore ain't got no sense nuh-now!"

After he let go of my arm, we stood there, quiet. He asked me if I needed any money.

"No."

"You shuh-shore?"

"I'm sure."

"All right," he said. "But you might nuh-need it."

"I might. And I might not."

"Buh-bright buh-boy," he told me. "Ain't got nuh-no choices, buh-but you nuh-know all thuh-the options."

I looked at the cypress stump clock on the wall. It was a quarter past two and I had gotten only a half hour of sleep, but I had to get going.

"Goodnight, Number One. Tell your folks thanks for letting us sleep here tonight."

"Buh-but you duh-didn't sleep."

"I slept some."

"Not enuh-nuh-nough. Little puh-pecker. You're

guh-gonna kuh-kill yourself, the wuh-way you luh-live. You and your buh-brother buh-both."

"Goodnight, Number One. Don't you worry about us."

"Your lips buh-bleeding."

"I know it."

As I walked to the door I heard him behind me, grumbling and shuffling his big sore feet. When I got past his driveway Number One shouted something at me I couldn't make out, so I told myself that it mustn't have been very important. I was sort of woozy, what with the thrashing I'd taken and everything, but I didn't have a hard time finding my way out of the air force base. You just took this road till it came to that road, and that road till it came to another, then you walked up to the guard, who saluted you, and there you were, back in the real world.

When I'd gotten there—to the real world, that is—I noticed how little things had changed. The Fort Seltrum Road was as broken as before, the ditches to the right and left stank with the same sewage and stillwater, and the sky above seemed just as full, loaded as ever for another mean rain.

On the way to my mother's house I fell into a bad habit I'd broken myself of long ago. When I walked, I didn't look at anything else except my feet. I kept my eyes pointed down all the time on the toes of my tennis shoes, and I didn't once look at the ditches, or the sky, or the road beneath me. My body felt so light I might not have had any feet at all, but I was moving toward my mother's house, as if something else were moving me.

———

After a while I fell out of my bad habit—I couldn't keep my eyes pinned to my feet if you paid me. They kept straying up, and drifting to the right or left, and if I did find the tolerance to keep them aimed low for more than a minute, my head would flood up black and dizzy, and my breathing would come so short I'd have to stop to catch my wind. I figured it was useless trying to keep them down if they had other intentions, so I let them roam freely, even though there wasn't that much around for them to see.

I headed north at the end of Fort Seltrum and came to a vacant lot before Limbeaux Street. Three kids about my age lay huddled on a mattress in the middle of the lot, sleeping despite the coming rain and general wetness. There were a couple of open cans of beans beside the mattress, and I picked one up to see if there were any beans left. I managed to finish off what little remained without waking any of the kids up, and I hurried off through the lot wondering what they were going to do when the harder rains of the morning came.

Limbeaux led directly to the parking lot of a shopping plaza where most of the stores had gone out of business. The only places still open were a movie theater and a pawn shop, a jewelry store and an automobile insurance agency. I kept to the walkway beneath the awnings of the separate stores, and when I came to the jewelry store I stared through the lit window.

In the back of the store a fat guard sat sleeping on a folding chair. There was a gun in his holster and a radio around his neck, and his hands hung twitching at his sides. Before him stood the display cases, rows upon rows of diamond jewelry. There were watches and necklaces and earrings and wedding rings, pendants and bracelets and glittering charms. A stone the size of a strawberry sat before me on a velvet cushion, and I pressed my head against the glass of the display case that protected it.

As soon as I had crossed the parking lot of the shopping plaza, I found myself standing before a ditch overflooded with stillwater. I could either walk an extra halfmile until the ditch ended or take off my shoes and wade across. I knew if I took the shortcut I might get hookworm, like my brother'd warned, but I couldn't tell whether I had the strength to walk another halfmile. Finally I decided that I'd try to find myself a plank of lumber, so I could stretch it across the ditch and use it as a walking bridge, but when I went to the backalley of the old shopping center I found nothing but broken glass and trash and wornout tires. As I walked back to the ditch my mind was made up for me when it began to rain overhead. It wasn't hard at first, but then, without warning, it started to squall.

I threw off my shirt and took off my shoes and held them both in my hands, then I waded into the ditch and felt its warmness run up to my chest. Beneath me the mud and sewage drew me down deeper with every footstep, and around me paper cups and old clothes floated in the rain-dimpled water. Halfway across I lost my footing, and the world became a wet brown bilgewater roar, but somehow I'd managed to keep my shirt and shoes dry. I emerged on the other side and rolled around in the grass to dry myself a bit, then I put my clothes back on. I could've stayed in the ditch and followed it all the way till I got there, but I found myself in a dirtalley that also led to my mother's house and his.

The dirtalley was bordered by a scrawny wire

fence and I took in the sights of the houses around me as
I ran shivering through the rain. Before one house I saw
a police car, the officer and some old man laughing out
loud in the street. In the backyard of another house a
dog stood tearing at a leather leash gathered in its jaws.
Its mouth worked broken and it whined like a child and
blood flowed in streams from beneath its nose. At one
squat house a lady sat swinging on a porchswing anchored by a backyard jungle gym. An unlit cigarette
hung from her mouth and her gingham dress was
soaked through from the hard pouring rain. When I
saw her I slowed down and waved at her and she
stubbed out her cigarette—which wasn't even lit—
gathered the hemline of her dress in her hands, waved
back at me, and walked quickly into her house. The
rain had died some so I stood at the wirefence and
watched the lady walk back inside. She had long brown
hair that fell below her bottom and her arms were as
thin as chinaberry twigs. As soon as she'd gotten into
her house a face appeared in her bedroom window. It
was a man, with a big bush of hair and a full beard and
dark brown eyes set in two sunken circles, and he was
scanning the backyard for signs of the lady. He looked
like he was crazy for her, and when he couldn't find any
trace of her his heavy eyes fell full and terrified. He
buried his face in his hands, and the curtains of the bedroom closed like wings over him, and I saw the
woman's hand run slowly and suddenly through the
patch of his hair. I knew then it would be all right for
him, and I stood there watching the man and woman
hold each other until the curtains had emptied themselves of their bodies.

From there it wasn't far to where my mother lived. The rain had died completely, and I trudged along slowly, my whole body itching from the dirtiness of the ditchwater. Maybe if she was nice she'd have a new set of clothes I could wear; maybe she'd take me in and run hot bathwater. But I wasn't counting on it. It was awfully late, and she'd probably be asleep in the same bed as him. I'd have to be careful to wake just her. If he caught sight of me, he might do to me what he'd done to my daddy. I didn't care none, though. He'd probably had his fill of slaughter.

A wooden stump split the dirtalley into two directions, and I took the path that bordered the ditch. It led me through some garbage barrels, and a stack of corrugated cardboard boxes, and when I saw the twittering light of a streetlamp I knew I'd reached the house where she lived. It was painted green and lit up funny by the light of the lamp, almost like a house in a cartoon. I jumped the fence that bordered their backyard and came to rest beneath the window of their bedroom. Maybe I could have been a little quieter, because I heard them discussing my arrival inside.

"Honey?"

"Huh . . ."

"Darlin', get up!"

"Wha . . . what is it? I don't wanna go there anym—"

"Quiet, honey! Listen. I heard something out there. I heard somebody at the fence. You've gotta get up and check it out."

"T'ain't nothin' . . . swear it . . .'s just yer 'magination's all."

I could hear the bed jiggling then, and the shadows of the bedroom window fled as a bedside lamp flickered on.

"No, it ain't my imagination. Now you get up!"

Disgusted, Bohannon grunted. The springs of the bed relaxed as he threw himself out of it. Above me, I could see the silhouette of my mother outlined in the white moonlight, and behind her I heard Bohannon cursing and grumbling.

"You want I should get the gun?"

"I don't know. Oh, do what you have to do!"

He slammed around through the dresser drawers for a while, then I heard my mother draw her breath.

"Where'd you get that, for Christ's sake?"

"Gun store." Something clicked. "It's my new toy."

Her silhouette at the window disappeared toward him.

"Do you really think you need all that?"

"You never know. Could be a big 'un."

She was all confidential whispers.

"You be careful with that thing."

"I will, I will. Now get on back in bed."

"You promise you'll be careful?"

"Oh, for the love of—! Yes, yes. I promise I'll be careful."

"Good." The bed sagged again as she got back into it; I could hear the springs. "As long as you promise."

The bedroom door slammed.

Quickly, I skittered away from the bedroom window and came to hide behind the weeds beneath the oil tank. He couldn't see me from where he was, but I could see him. He came out to the backyard holding that toy of his, the kind of thing a wildman would own, and he used it sort of as a walking stick as he surveyed the tool shed, the garbage cans, and pine trees. If there'd been a burglar, Bohannon would've been easy enough to see, the backyard being so well lit and all, but he was rather lackadaisical about his whole approach. Bohannon twirled the gun around like a baton, let it slip from his hands once or twice, used it like a broom handle to knock down a couple of hornets' nests, and hooked it behind his shoulders and hung swinging from the clotheswire like an overstuffed scarecrow. Satisfied that my mama'd been imagining everything, he sauntered back into the house, and when he'd disappeared from view I hurried back to my position beneath their window.

My mother was quiet for a minute. Then she said, "You shore you didn't see nobody nowhere?"

Bohannon sighed. "Yes. God, yes. I'm posolutely absitive."

"Good," my mama said. The springs moaned as she lay back down.

I did not move.

"Honey?"

"What."

Their bedroom light was out now.

"I was just thinking."

"Uh-hum."

"I was thinking and—" She gathered her breath. "Well. Maybe it was him we heard outside."

At that, Bohannon rolled over; I could hear his body turn.

"Awww, baby! Why'd you have to go and—"

She was crying. "I know!" she sobbed. "Oh, don't I

know?" She said a whole bunch of things then, things I could barely understand, about how she was worried and she knew she shouldn't be, about how he was such a crazy fool and would try anything, about how she feared for her darling's life after what he'd done. I could tell from the noises the bedcovers made that Bohannon was holding her, trying to calm her down. His voice kept saying "Shhh!"; his baby didn't have to be afraid of anything; she'd be safe as long as he was there to protect her; they'd get everything that was coming to them if only they let life play itself out proper. It was sort of sad listening in—my mother's voice so hard and broken, Bohannon trying to stay sweet and encouraging—and I knew from the tone of my mama's voice that there was nothing Bohannon could say, nothing a fella could do. In the quiet of the night my mama's sobbing rose from a whisper to a moan. The lights of the house next door came on, and I spied an old man sticking his nose through two pink curtains. All the while poor Bohannon kept saying, "Shhh! Shhh, baby!", and the sheets whispered as he held her.

It did not take much courage for me to knock at the door. It would've taken courage to have walked away, but I was afraid. I knocked at the door.

He answered.

"Why, it's you!" he said. He did not seem awake enough to be angry. "What're you doing here at this time of the night?"

"I'd like to see my mama."

"Hold on," he told me. "Wait one minute. I'll get her."

He had not asked me in and I was happy of that and in no time at all she appeared at the door, dressed in a blue robe, eyes smudged with tears and tapwater.

"What're you doing here?"

"I don't know."

She took me by the wrist and tried to lead me into the house, but I wouldn't budge.

"All right," she said. "You do what you want."

A long silence unraveled in which I didn't know what to say and stood looking at the ground. She didn't know what to say, either, and I supposed had I looked up she would've been looking at the ground herself. When I did look up I saw Bohannon in the kitchen window scooting around making a pot of coffee. He looked like he'd been licking a sore tail.

"Well," I said, "I best be going."

I turned to leave and she called out to me.

"Yes'm?"

She bit one of her nails.

"Come here."

"What, ma'am?" I asked her.

"I said, 'Come here.'"

She closed the frontdoor behind her and squatted on the porch and held out her arms, and I went to her and let her take me. She said my name over and over in a way I hadn't heard it said before and she smelled like warm soap and I didn't want her to let go. With her free hand she stroked my hair.

"Honey?"

"Yes'm."

"Did he send you here?"

"Who?"

"Your daddy."

"My daddy?"

"Yes."

I shook my head.

"No'm."

She sighed, deep.

"Then why're you here?"

"I don't know, ma'am."

"Yes," she said, laughing. "You told me that already."

She stopped stroking my hair and held me at arm's length.

"Ma'am?" I said. I thought she wanted to ask me a question.

She coughed.

"You said you don't know why you're here."

"That's right," I told her.

She stared into me.

"Why don't you know why you're here?"

I closed my eyes.

"I don't know. You know why you're here?"

She smiled, and I felt like I'd been baited.

"Yes," she said. "To take care of you."

I tried to look away, but her eyes held me fast.

"That's nice," I told her. "But Daddy can take care of me."

"Can he?"

"Yes'm."

She touched my eye with her finger. It stung.

"Is he the one who took care of your eye there? Is he the one who took care of your lip?"

"No'm." I told her it was him that hit me, not Daddy, not this time.

She bowed her head.

"I don't believe it."

"You don't have to."

She touched my torn lip with her littlest finger.

"No, I don't. I *don't* have to, do I?"

When she let go of me I shoved my hands in my pockets. We looked each other over good but didn't say much of anything.

"You gon' come in?"

"No, ma'am. Thank you."

She bit her thumb.

"All right," she said. "All right."

After a while I said I had to go. She asked me if I'd seen my brother.

"Yes'm."

"When?"

"Couple hours ago."

"Where is he now?"

"With Daddy, I 'spect."

"With your father?" she asked.

"Yes'm," I told her. "With Daddy."

She stood to go inside and I started off to leave, but just as the frontdoor was about to shut I heard footsteps falling toward me.

"Darling!" she called. "Come 'ere now. Be sweet to your mother and come on over here!"

I let her hold me again; I didn't mind.

"Honey," she said to me, whispering, petting my hair, "if your brother decides to come live with us, would you want to come and stay with us too?"

"I don't know," I said. I mentioned my brother's name. "Did he say he was gonna?"

"No, dear. Not yet. But he will, I just know it!"

She was holding me very tight.

"Are you sure he will?"

She nodded her head. I could see Bohannon staring at us through the kitchen window.

"Yes!" she said. "I'm just sure of it!"

I shook my head, slowly, drew myself away from her. My face felt flushed, and things were going fast.

"I don't think he'll stay with you, Mama."

"How do you know, darlin'? How can you know?"

I shook my head, faster now. "He won't," I said. "I just know him. I think he'd rather die than live in this house, Mama. And he's with Daddy now. Like me. I'm not saying that's right, but I know that's how it is. And besides, I don't think it's his choice."

She looked at me funny then, like I was speaking some kind of language that was foreign to her. "What do you mean, 'his choice'? What do you mean by that?"

I took a few steps backwards, beyond her. I was trying not to lose myself. "I'm not sure," I said. "But I know it's the truth, that we ain't got no choice and we're with Daddy now, that we ain't had no choice from the beginning, now, or ever. We'd come to you, maybe, but we couldn't if we wanted to. I'm not sure what it all means, but it's the truth, all of it!"

She had that look about her, the look of someone who's been spun around on a playground swing one too many turns. She held out her arms, as if she needed something to steady her, but I stood still.

"In a lot of ways," she told me, "you're just like your daddy."

"Our daddy," I told her.

She went inside.

———

I looked at the night and wondered if maybe it wasn't too late to head back home.

Daddy might be sleeping, and him too. With both of them dead out, I could rest myself behind the davenport where neither of them would think to look come the morning. It was a comforting thought, me stretched out on the pee-smelling pile of the living room rug, safe in the shadows where no one could see me. I certainly was tired enough. The last time I'd really slept was more than twenty-four hours ago, and though I'd been knocked out twice during that period of time, I couldn't bring myself to calling it sleep.

A clean cold nightwind blew straight through me and above me the sky hung wasted and unspent. Through the darkness I could see a gray patchwork of clouds, the last of the evening gathering together, and I knew that before the early morning broke there'd be one last storm less merciful than its brothers.

My chest heaved like a rusted whistle and I felt my forehead and found I had a fever. It must've been all the ditchcrossing, and running, and living off nothing but sandwiches and Gatorade. Of course, getting hit in the chest and stomach a couple dozen times didn't help matters neither, but my sickness was nothing sleep couldn't cure.

I took the quickest route to getting home there was—through the playground at Ulysses S. Grant, down Dellray Road to the Vale of Tears Funeral Home, through the home's backlot to the West Rail gas station, and past the West Rail onto Pennymont Boulevard. It

was a good two miles' walk, and my head was light. I
hoped that I'd make it.

Ulysses S. Grant was a day school for rich kids that
wasn't in operation no more. A bunch of men had set
fire to it a couple of years back when the school had been
out of session, and all the buildings with the exception of
the library had burned to the ground. A man and his
wife from the north had founded the school. They only
took about fifty kids a year, but they swore they'd give
them the best education money could buy, and supposedly they had. My mother wanted me to go there,
but we couldn't afford it, and whenever we told our
daddy we were going to the Ulysses S. Grant playground to play, he'd wrinkle his nose like somebody'd
cut the cheese. A lot of folks didn't like the school much,
and I supposed that was why they'd let it burn down.
Some folks even claimed that the northern couple had
planned it, that the school had been a failure and they'd
wanted the insurance on it, but after the place got
torched I noticed that they hadn't stuck around to collect whatever was coming to them.

Even though Ulysses was fried and all, my brother
and I liked to scavenge through it. My favorite place was
the library. It was only partially burnt, and a lot of
neighborhood folks had looted chairs and desks and library curtains, but most of the books still sat on the
shelves. I'd climb in through one of the busted windows,
grab an armful, and sit outside the library reading them;
I'd always return them even though I could have taken
them home with me, so it was just like a regular library.
My favorite book was about a lightning bug that scribbled messages in the sky to warn people of coming danger. The messages looked like chain lightning, and they

saved the lives of little kids who played in night traffic
or hung around railroad tracks or slept on roofs in thun
derstorms or whatever. My brother liked this one book
about Benjamin Franklin because of the pictures, but I
looked at the writing and it weren't no good.

At night the grounds of Ulysses lay like a sleeping
man who'd been set on fire. Its arms and legs were ash,
and its burnt-out body was black broken rubble. You
could see the limbs of chairs and desks sticking out of
windows like upended children, and across the brown
weed-eaten ground a layer of glass glimmered dimly in
the moonlight.

I didn't stop to do any adventuring, but as I walked
by I did chance to look through the window of one classroom that wasn't as damaged as the others. There were
a couple of uncharred desks, and a blackboard stretched
from one end of the far wall to the other. I could tell
some neighborhood kids had decided to make a club-
house of the classroom because there were dirty words
written on the chalkboard and someone had spray-
painted a skull and crossbones across the American flag.
It was a pretty decent skeleton, and you could barely see
the blood of the flag for all the ivory bones.

Once past the schoolgrounds I came to Dellray.
Though I knew a policeman might see me, I stuck to the
sidewalk. I'd checked my face in one of the Ulysses windows and noticed that the ditchwater had washed most
of my cuts clean, so I wasn't bleeding as much anymore.
The only noticeable thing was my black eye, and if a cop
stopped to ask me how I'd gotten it, I'd tell him the
truth. To arrest my brother he'd have to find him first;
and it wasn't like most cops to come between family.

Dellray led to the Vale of Tears Funeral Home. It

was a box-shaped building with signs around the parking lot that read "Visitors Only." I took to the side alley of the building and found my path blocked by the light of an open window. Someone was singing, and I was afraid that if I passed by they might take me for a grave-robber and shoot me and salt me. I crept to the window and got some kind of orange crate and stepped up on it and peered above the sill. I wanted to see what I was up against.

Two large Spanish women were leaning over what looked like a metal dinner table. One of them had a canvas bag of makeup strapped around her shoulder, and the other one kept stepping back and squinting her eye. Their hands worked the whole while, busy on something I couldn't see. Every now and then they'd stop their singing to tell each other stories. I supposed they were telling jokes because whenever the stories finished the women'd throw up their hands and hug each other madly and huge laughing tears would roll down their faces. They were too occupied to notice me passing by, so I left as quick as I'd come and jumped the fence that separated the Vale of Tears from the West Rail backlot. I heard them singing a song again, something about "la luna, la luna."

The West Rail was an all-night filling station owned by a young guy named Wilson. He always dressed like an ice-cream man, in white cotton trousers and a white Oxford shirt, but that's not to say he didn't look good. He was sharp all-around, Wilson was, and folks often wondered what a guy like that was doing working at a dirty old gas station. He had a winning way about him—didn't smoke or cuss but didn't mind folks who did—and whatever time of the day you saw

him, whether early in the morning or late at night, he'd
be sitting in a lawn chair outside the station office with a
book the size of a cinder block sitting in his lap. He was
awful smart, and made good conversation, and he kept
his blond hair greased and parted down the middle so it
fell in two long V-shaped flaps over the sockets of his
eyes. His only trouble was he didn't pay enough attention to what was going on around him, and a lot of times
when you talked to him you had to repeat yourself till
you were blue in the face. But that didn't matter none to
me. Even though Wilson was a lot different from other
folks, there wasn't nobody I'd rather get bluegilled talking to.

From the corner of the station I could see him sitting in his old familiar spot, dressed in his new shirt and
pants in his old familiar fashion. A can of Off! sat
propped atop a six-pack beside his chair, and I couldn't
see the title of the book in his lap, though I squinted.
Wilson himself was busy poring through it, his round
reading glasses on the crooked tip of his nose, and all
around his head moths and nightflies formed a sort of
buzzing halo. A gray stream of hosewater ran below
Wilson's chair and over Wilson's naked feet, and I could
see his tan deckshoes on a nearby vending machine.
From somewhere in the background a radio played, and
though I noticed Wilson's lips were moving I didn't
know whether they were moving with what he happened to be reading, or whether he was singing along to
the radio station. Knowing Wilson, it was probably
something altogether different. He was the kind of fella
who thought better three ways than most did one.

I was tempted to stay and shoot the breeze with
him, but I didn't want him to see me looking so punk.

He might get worried and try to take me to the hospital
or something; he was that type. So I stood behind the
edge of the shop and watched him read awhile, waiting
for him to maybe doze off a little, but he didn't show any
signs. Now and then he'd rub his eyes slow and hard
with his hands all balled up into fists, close his book, and
stare off into the distance with a heartbreak look that
could drown an orphan in her own tears. I wondered if
he was the type of person who didn't need sleep, or
maybe the type of person who needed it but couldn't
get it.

While I was watching him, a woman in a beat-up
Chevy pulled in and filled up her tank. She walked over
to Wilson smiling and wiping her forehead with a
handkerchief. Wilson grinned at her and took her
money and said wasn't it a hot night for the rain and
everything. She said yes sir, it sure was, but didn't he
look like he had it beat? She pointed to the six-pack of
beer by his side and he laughed and picked one up and
handed the sweating bottle to her. She took it and said
thank you and now she knew where to come to at three-
thirty in the morning when she wanted a cheap tank of
gas and a cold bottle of beer. Wilson said maybe the gas
wasn't so cheap and the beer not so cold, but she could
come back any time as far as he was concerned. She
blushed a little at that and said thank you again and
good night, and she drove off in her Chevy which
looked like it might not make it around the next street-
corner. As soon as the lady'd pulled away, a trucker in a
big diesel came in behind her. He was a strapping guy
with wild red hair and he swung his rig to the side of the
pump, put it in park, slammed the cardoor with a bang,
and skipped half-walking half-running on over to

Wilson. How-do, Wilson told him, and took his credit
card. Just sweet, the trucker said, couldn't be better. He
was on an eighteen-hour run to the capital and back,
and if he made it in fifteen, he said, bouncing up and
down on his heels like it was cold out, he'd get a two-
hundred-dollar bonus. Wilson said that sounded like a
tough run, but he wished him all the luck in the world.
When he'd finished with the trucker's credit card,
Wilson bent over to offer the man a bottle of beer, but
the trucker held up his hand. Union rules, he said, then
folded his arms against the side of his head to show
Wilson how drinking beer put him to sleep. Wilson
laughed and told him all right, all right, he wasn't the
type to put a beer between a trucker and two hundred
dollars. The trucker smiled, took back his credit card,
said thanks for everything, and pumped Wilson's hand
like a maniac. Then he half-walked half-ran back to his
rig and filled her with gas. I wondered why Wilson
hadn't made the trucker pump before he'd paid like he
had the lady, but I supposed Wilson was the type to trust
everybody for any reason, to let them pump gas and pay
for it in whatever order suited them best.

As soon as the trucker had filled his tank and
pulled away, Wilson stood and stretched and waved
away the bugs and moths around his head and went into
his office to turn up the radio. Springsteen was on, and I
would've turned it up too. While he was in there I proceeded to head off across the station lot as calm as I
could so's to keep from attracting Wilson's attention,
but it was awfully dark at the West Rail. The big neon
WR sign had burnt out about a week ago, and as I
walked across the lot my foot tread across the rubber
tube that rung the bell that told Wilson he had a cus-

tomer. Sure enough, he saw me, and when he called out my name, what else could I do?

"Hello, you!" Wilson shouted, flailing his arms.

I went over to him.

"Hey there, Wilson. How's it going? Me, I was just out walking around. Fell down and scraped myself up nasty there a while back. What do you think of this rain? Gee, she's funny, ain't she?"

Wilson stood cockeyed, staring at my cuts and bruises.

"You must a fell down pretty good there."

"Oh, I did! Boy, you should've seen me. Fell right down. Was a regular more-on!"

He scratched his jaw and ran his fingers around beneath his collar, sizing me up. At last he shook his head and laughed and flopped back down in his lawn chair, satisfied that whatever fist I fell down on or into was my affair and mine alone.

"Yeah, well. Haw haw haw. I've fallen down a few times in my day too. Yes sir!" He bent over and picked up a beer. "You want one of these here—oh now hold it. I forgot. You're a little too young now, ain't you? Almost did something I shouldn't've," he said. "Haw haw haw!" He put the beer back down with the rest of the six-pack, straightened the book on his lap, and cleared his throat. "Oh, this weather shore is something. Can you believe her? I ain't never seen nothing like her. Hey? You know what?"

"What?"

"You're just in time." He stood up and went to his

office and came back with two pairs of sunglasses. He
gave me one. "Put them on."

"Why?"

"Now, now. You just do like I tell you and put
them on. There's gonna be an eclipse." He got up again
and went around to the side of the building and came
back with another lawn chair. "Take a load off," he
said. I did. When I was comfortable he sat down in his
chair and put on his shades. "I look like a real dude," he
grinned. "Don't I?" I laughed a little and told him he
did. He nodded and swallowed and slumped down
with his arms stretched out behind him. Half-sitting,
half-lying there, he rested in the chair, star-gazing. "I
remember my first eclipse," he said. "I was about your
age then. Nineteen something or other, it isn't important. The week before it came, people couldn't stop talking about it. Total solar eclipse. It was in the papers and
on television. Don't look directly at it, folks said. It'll
blind you for life. I remember there were barkers on
streetcorners selling special solar eclipse sunglasses for,
say, ten dollars a shot. Who had that kind of money?
Most everyone was asleep when the eclipse came anyway. But my sister and me, I remember, we sat on the
roof of our house until four o'clock in the morning, just
waiting for the fool thing to show."

I straightened my sunglasses. "Did it?"

Wilson looked at me.

"Did it what?"

I looked at him.

"Did it show?"

"Oh!" Wilson said. He laughed and picked up a
bottle of beer. He looked at it for a while, then put it

back down. "Yeah, it showed. Sure it did. You can't hide an eclipse."

Wilson was very quiet then. The whole world was. "Wilson?"

"What's that? What'd you say?"

I sat up in my seat. "I can't be staying long. What time does the thing show?"

He stared at me, confused. He took off his sunglasses and fiddled with the pagemarker in his book. "What thing? What do you mean, thing?"

I shook my head. "Your eclipse."

"Oh!" Wilson said, chuckling. "That's right. Er, well—" He cleared his throat and counted on his fingers. "I'd say about, uh, two hours and a half. That ain't long, but of course if you've got to go." He bent over to pick up a bottle of beer, then stared at his hand and laughed. "There I go again! Haw haw haw!" He put the beer back down and cleared his throat. "You're in for a real treat, you are. It's not every day that you get to see a meteor shower."

I stared at him. "Meteor shower?"

"How's that?"

"You just said meteor shower. I thought there was going to be an eclipse?"

"What's that, meteor shower? Who said that? I didn't say anything about no eclipse. Hey!—What happened to your face there, buddy? You're all beat up!"

Wilson sweated heavily through his clothes, and his eyes were ticking nervously. I wanted to tell him that I'd fallen down, but I remembered how I'd told him that already. It wasn't important, I supposed. Wilson was Wilson. You could take him or leave him. When a man in a station wagon pulled up at the full-service island, Wilson told me to help myself to whatever beer I wanted and hurried off to help the customer. The customer looked Wilson up and down when he arrived to pump gas, and you could tell Wilson had made some kind of an impression. He sure was respectable looking in his white ice-cream suit. The customer didn't even notice his bare feet and wriggling toes. He just stood there looking him over and grinning from ear to ear. It's not every day that a sharp guy like Wilson pumps your gas.

The customer paid and left and Wilson came back over and sat down. I got up.

"What's this? Are you leaving? Hey now—you just got here."

"I know," I told him. "But I've got to go."

He ran his fingers back under his collar, looking me over with that helpless way of his. "You don't have to go. Or do you? Well, well, well. Want a beer?"

He picked one up and held it out to me. I took it and said goodbye. As I was walking away he called out to me.

"Hey! Ain't you gonna wait and see the comet?"

I told him no, I was gonna go home and sit on my roof and watch it. And sure enough, when I got home, who did I see sitting there on our roof but my brother. I climbed up and said hello.

"Quiet," he told me. "Comet's coming."

"Comet's coming?"

"That's what I said."

"Wilson tell you that?"

"Who's Wilson?"

He looked me over and noticed the bottle of beer in my hand.

"Give me that."

"All right."

"Come on and give it."

"I said I would."

Because we were on the slanted part of the roof I had to hobble up an incline to reach where my brother sat. I handed him the beer and he screwed off the top.

"Welcome," I said.

"For what?" He looked at me sort of wild. "You're welcome for what?"

"Nothing."

He turned back around to where he'd been look-ing, a long line of trees cut black against the night. It was almost pitch dark where my brother was sitting, and I couldn't tell whether he'd gone inside to clean himself off or not. He also seemed to have forgotten all about the working over he'd given me. He didn't act in the least bit sorry.

I said his name.

He winced.

"What?"

"You seen Daddy yet?"

"Daddy?"

He repeated the word like he'd never heard it before.

"Daddy?"

I told him yeah. "You been in to see him yet?"

As he sat in the darkness on the crown of the roof he kept his back turned to me, so it was hard to tell exactly what he was doing. I saw his head sort of fall down low to his chest and his whole body started to quiver and chill. His arms rose and fell at his sides like nervy wings, and he brought them to rest twitching against his chest. His teeth made a steady chattering noise, like bones rattling or knuckles cracking or someone knocking at somebody's door in the middle of the morning or night, and a hysterical song, like the noise of anyone passing away, rose from my brother's throat. I thought he was laughing at first, as if I'd asked some ridiculous question, but from the way he shook I knew it was more than laughter. From far across the city I heard a siren screaming, and the screaming grew steadily louder as it neared, then less and less severe as it disappeared away. My brother fumbled about for something in the pocket of his pants—his medicine, I thought, or maybe one of the cigarettes from the fresh pack I'd stolen for him. But what he pulled out was neither of these. It was a knife, thin and curved, and it sparkled in whatever light fell across our patched roof. My brother held it tight in his balled-up hand and pounded it hard against the tar, his soft hysterical music growing more and more quiet with the rhythm of his beating.

"Where'd you find that knife?" I asked.

He did not answer me. He fumbled for the bottle of beer he'd put between his legs, and when he found it he took a swig, wiped his mouth, and settled the bottle back on the slanted roof. It toppled over and he caught it and a stream of beer ran down in a line across the tar. There wasn't much beer left in the bottle, so he hurled it into the backyard and it shattered against a fencepost. I asked the question again.

"Where'd you find that knife there? It's a nice one."

He shrugged stupidly and shoved the knife back in his pocket.

"Daddy guv it to me."

"So you've seen him?"

"Yes, I've seen him."

His back kept turned.

"What's he been doin'?"

"Sleeping."

"Did you wake him?"

"No."

"Is he sleeping now?"

He started to shake again.

"I don't know. No. Wait. I, I don't think—"

I wanted to get closer to him so I could understand better what he was saying, but I was afraid to get too altogether near him, what with the knife he had and everything. He sounded like he was still gone on his medicine, and I wondered if he'd gotten any more from our daddy. I said his name again.

"Stop it. Stop saying that."

I was quiet for a little while, then I asked him about the medicine.

"No," he said. "I didn't get any. Daddy'd gone and drunk it all."

He drew the knife back out of his pocket and began to write words he couldn't read on the bumpy tar roof. As he moved the knife in the dim light I could see long smears of red on the blade. I wanted to ask him how they'd gotten there, but I was afraid to. From the way he'd been talking I knew his head wasn't very much with him.

"Can I see your knife?"

"See it with your eyes," he said.

All the while I'd been there he'd only looked at me once, and when he had it was as if he'd been ashamed to. He kept his back to me, and though his sad singing had stopped, every couple seconds his body would bunch up and shiver like a snake uncoiling. He acted like maybe he was sick or worse. I remembered the time our daddy'd said that in the end you can't be any sicker than dead.

"Have you gone in to see him yet?"

It was him talking this time.

"No," I said. "You want I should climb down and—"

"No!"

He was up now, standing before me, the slanted roof adding to his height and the long knife glittering against the crooked sky. He was more in the light than he'd been before, and I could see how wet with blood he was. I went so far as to reach out and touch him. Sure enough, he was slick with it.

"I killed a man," he told me.

I didn't believe it.

"You're just talking."

"Like hell I am."

"Who was it?" I asked him. "Some old drunk?"

He looked at me and smiled. "That's it exactly."

The next thing I knew he was scaling down the trellis, the one that hung beside our daddy's bedroom window. As I followed my brother I peered through the curtains into my daddy's dim-lit room and saw him lying on his back half-off the bed. He looked about as dead to the world as I'd ever seen him, but at least he was so gone he couldn't hear us.

"Did you really kill a man?" I said.

My brother and me were in the tool shed now. He was banging around for something or other.

"I told you I did," he answered, not looking at me. "An old drunk. Like the type that huddles each night on Caritas. He tried to knock me down, tried to hurt me, and I had this old knife Daddy guv me. I didn't want to kill him, but you know."

I reached out my hand and touched the wet blood again.

"You just killed a dog or something, didn't you?"

He looked at me, looked through me.

"Believe what you want," he said.

I followed him through the backyard and out onto the street. A ball of light fell across the sky, and a whip of wind tousled my brother's hair.

"Where are we going?" I asked.

"I'm going to your mama's house."

I told him I'd just been there.

"Liar!" he swore. "You lie like a rug!"

I told him it was the truth, but he said he was sick of all my lying.

"Why don't you just head back on home?" he told me. "Why don't you stop all your following me around? If you've been to her house once already tonight, why don't you just butt the hell out of it?"

When I said I would, that I was sick of following him halfdead and bloody all across town in the middle of the night, that I'd go right home and tell Daddy where he was going, and what he'd been doing, he practically begged me not to leave. He needed me, he said, at least for a little while. He hadn't really killed a man, see. All the blood was from him wounding a part of himself, on account of he was so mad at not having any medicine. He was real weak and needed someone to look after him, and couldn't I see from all the blood that he wasn't in no shape to be left alone?

"You're fine," I told him. "You don't need nobody. All you are is blood, and no matter how much there is of it you don't stop moving none. You ain't hurt any, so far as I can see. You probably went fishing and cleaned a fish with that knife. You didn't kill no drunk, and you didn't hurt yourself. Even if you did, how would I know? You're made out of blood. It's all you are. You're bloody all the goddamn time."

When I finished talking he started to bluster, cursing me to high heaven and telling me to go back home to my daddy if I wanted to. He worked himself up into a regular lather, and at last he made a run at me with his knife. He caught me too, and sat straddled over me with the knife in between his chest and mine. He was crying, hard.

"I did too kill a man!" he shouted, sobbing. "I did too kill him! Please believe me? Please?"

Slowly, then, the knife fell from my brother's hand. His whole body seemed to give, and he rolled off of me, crying. I stood from where I'd been, covered in the blood of my brother like I'd been hours before, and I stared at him curled up and moaning on the grass. When he'd recovered and we were walking again, I asked him if he wanted me to carry the can of gasoline he'd taken from the tool shed.

"No," he said. "I got it. I got it."

He really had killed a man. It was true, every bit of it.

———

There was nothing either of us could do now except wait and see what the death of the night brought.

I looked at my brother. He seemed to have the vision of a tom. He kept his head fixed straight ahead of him, eyelids flinching and neck muscles twitching with the rush of every passing car. We must have made a gory pair, and I wondered what the folks on Pennymont thought of us. Were it Halloween, they might have thought the dead were walking the earth. Maybe it didn't have to be Halloween for them to think that.

"So you saw Daddy?"

"Yes."

"Did you talk to him?"

He nodded.

In my brother's condition making conversation was like pulling teeth, so I settled myself with the silence of the darkness and kept my eyes on him in case he strayed into the road. He was walking awfully funny, almost like he'd forgotten how. He'd take one step with his right foot, then maybe two and a half with his left. He didn't fall over or anything, though I wondered how he kept his balance. I thought at first he was just being funny. I even laughed at him. But when he kept doing it, not even looking down to see whether his feet were for or against him, I didn't laugh no more. As rigs rolled by he had the tendency to drift nearer and nearer the road, and I had to walk behind him, punching him now and then at the base of his spine to keep him from drifting head on into traffic. Had I not been there, he wouldn't have either. He needed me more than even he knew.

We walked by the West Rail and I couldn't see any sign of Wilson anywhere. It was for the best, I supposed.

It he'd seen the both of us in our condition he might have gotten a bit suspicious. The gasoline can in my brother's hand was enough, I thought, to pique Wilson's curiosity. But wherever he was we were out of his sight.

My brother took advantage of the situation and ran half-stumbling into Wilson's office. He emerged without being seen, his canteen jostling with brand new medicine, and tossed me a couple candy bars. In his hand he held a box of matches, and I knew why he hadn't been smoking the pack of cigarettes I'd stolen for him earlier. There'd been nothing to light them with.

He handed me the can of gasoline and fumbled around in his pockets for the cigarettes. Finding them, he tore the red seal and drew one out. Though his hands were shaking he managed to get one of the matches in the matchbox lit, and he stared at the flame for a couple of seconds before putting it to the tip of his cigarette. Having a smoke seemed to clear his head. His walking perked up as we rounded the corner that led to the backlot of the West Rail, and the sound of Wilson's sleepless laughter hit us as we reached the fence.

"You there! Up here! That's right, on the roof!"

A yellow wooden ladder stood leaning against the back wall of the filling station, and on the very top rung I saw Wilson's feet dangling. The pantlegs of his white cotton trousers were cuffed up, revealing his knobby ankles, and a pair of binoculars hung down in front of his crotch. The rest of Wilson was invisible in the darkness, but his loony laughter and kicking legs were enough to hold our attention.

"You!" he hollered. "You two! Don't act like you can't see me! I'm right where you think I am! If you'd just get your duffs off that ground down there, you

could come up here and see the most incredible show!
Comets, an eclipse, meteor showers! I even got binoculars so you can see the action close up!" He jiggled
the binoculars to show he meant business. "In an hour
or two it's going to be daylight, and all the miracles of
the night'll be gone! So come on, now! I'm not going to
beg you no longer! You'll see it all better from up here
anyhow! It's darker!"

My brother began to climb the fence. I followed.
Wilson kept haranguing us about all the meteors and
miracles we were missing, and my brother took the cigarette out of his mouth, held it in his fist, and shook it at
Wilson. "You be quiet up there!" he shouted. "I already
seen the comet, and all them other things too! So hush
up your laughing and leave us be!"

Wilson was quiet then, and his legs disappeared
from the top of the ladder. I reached the highest point of
the fence and stared up at the sky. It was dull, and black,
and overhung by clouds that looked like the dirty skirts
of women, and I couldn't see any of the things that
Wilson was jawing about. Maybe he was right, maybe
you did need binoculars; maybe you did need to be on
higher ground. Either way my brother and I were out of
luck. We didn't have any binoculars nor the time to go
crawling up on any more roofs. The comets and meteors
and total eclipses would have to content themselves with
looking at us.

I leapt from the fence and turned to hear a mighty
crash. The ladder to the roof of the West Rail had collapsed and splintered on the backlot. Wilson would be
trapped until the morning, unless he had the humility to
call to one of his customers for help.

I took to the side alley of the Vale of Tears and

came upon my brother staring in the same window I'd stared in before. The Spanish women were busy at work, telling one another stories and singing "la luna, la luna." My brother asked me what they were doing.

"Salting somebody down," I said.

He looked at me in horror.

"No."

I nodded.

"Yes they are. It's the truth."

I hopped on the orange crate I'd left there before, and my brother blew smoke through the open window. The Spanish women caught wind of it and turned their heads to look at us. The larger one made a spoiled-milk face and shook her finger at us, as if to say, "This isn't the type of place for boys like you to be hanging around." The other one folded her arms across her chest and made a "tsk tsk tsk" noise with her mouth. It was clear that they wanted the both of us to leave, but my brother wouldn't, so neither would I.

"What are ya doing?" he asked them.

They looked at each other and shook their heads.

"Hey, señoritas, what's that you're doing? Who's 'at on the metal slab there?"

The larger woman leaned over and whispered something in her companion's ear. The companion took a step back and looked at her larger friend and jiggled with laughter and patted the woman naughtily on the cheek. She reached into her makeup bag and took out a tube of lipstick and turned it until a red point showed. Then she asked my brother and me something neither of us could understand because we didn't speak Spanish. Nevertheless, whatever the question was, my brother answered yes.

"*Sí,* señorita," he told the women, grinning like a goat. He stubbed out his cigarette on the ledge of the windowsill. "*Sí,* señorita. *Sí, sí, sí.*"

Slowly, without an inch of expression on her face, the smaller woman stepped toward us. The tube of lipstick hung at her side. When she reached the open window she took my brother's head in her hands, made a small red "x" on his forehead, and kissed him on the mouth. It was like a ceremony.

My brother said, "Do him too." He pointed at me. "Do him too."

Unwilling, the smaller woman called her larger friend, but she waved her hands and refused to come over. The smaller woman looked back at us and shrugged and turned and walked away, but my brother's eyes would not leave her. She remained out of sight for a good long minute, then returned at last and walked over to us and drew a heavy curtain between us and the slabroom. Soon, from inside, a wicked roar of laughter came, and my brother touched the red mark on his forehead. He rubbed it between his fingers.

"Did you see that?" he whispered. "Did you see it? Did you?"

Now we were heading back down Dellray to where my mother lived with Bohannon. Nothing was said about our going there or what we were going to do once we arrived, but we headed in that direction nonetheless. I kept trying to make talk with my brother—he was in such a deadfaced mood—but he wouldn't have none of it, so after a while I gave up. I could've told him Lucifer was behind him with a red-hot poker and he

wouldn't've listened, and it scared me to be around anybody who'd given up so completely on talk.

All the while we walked I stayed a good bit behind
him, maybe four or five feet, to keep him from hurting
himself like before. There were more cars now as the
morning came on, but Dellray took a lot of traffic no
matter what the time of night. As cars passed by, my
brother reached for the eyes of the drivers, reached for
them with his eyes, which were bloodless and tired and
cold. Sometimes he'd reach a driver's eyes so good the
cars would drift suddenly in our direction. My brother
was like a hypnotist—though if I were driving and saw
some kid in my brother's shape, covered in guts, hag-
gard, stumbling like a flesh-and-blood mannequin in
the early morning darkness on a dirty city sideroad, I
might have lost control too.

My brother was some sight. With a cigarette in one
hand and a rusty can of gasoline in the other, his canteen
bulging from his bloody army jacket, he nearly took the
kick out of your heart. But I was used to him, used to
him like you might get used to a guy with one arm or a
crying dog or an old man that coughs and spits in good
company. There was no need to worry because there
wasn't any way to change his circumstances, and though
I could've turned tail and walked away, that wouldn't
have dried the blood on his skin, or cleared the curious
odor from his tongue, or filled up that look of the dead
in his eyes.

Summer was closing shop that time of the year,
and the mornings carried a sharpness to them. It might
have been the air that made my brother shiver, but as we
came toward the last four blocks of Dellray, I remembered the other times my brother and I'd attempted to

check out the house where my mama was staying, how he'd get sick halfway there. His body would bend and he'd breathe quick and sweat would rise up on his skin like dew. He'd have to hug his stomach and clamp his mouth shut to keep from chucking up, and we'd always turn around and head back from where we came. So it was amazing that we'd gotten as far as we had, and I wasn't surprised at the way he stopped dead when I pointed to our mama's house and told him it was hers.

"That one right there?"

"That's right."

He drew out his canteen and put it to his lips and tipped it up. I watched his Adam's apple seesaw and knew he'd drunk the whole thing down. When he'd finished he didn't put the canteen back in his jacket; he let it fall to the road with a hollow clang. I went to it and picked it up for him, but he grabbed it out of my hand and took a running start and cursed and punted it like a football. As he swung back around to face me his eyes swelled up with a helpless look as if the floor of the earth had given out from underneath him. His knees buckled and he fell to the ground, looking like a man on a brittle float of ice, and the mouth of the night gaped black like a whirlpool, determined and bent on swallowing him whole. I watched him curled up and shaking from a distance. I watched him without comment while the cars passed by.

My brother had this thing about dying. It was a thing everybody had, but I supposed he had it more than others.

When we were little our daddy would leave us in the house with the front and backdoors bolted from out-side. He also left food around, so we could eat. It hap-

pened when our mama went up north for a whole
winter to visit her kin in Panama City. We'd had a lady
to stay with us, but Daddy drove her off. Instead of
hiring another woman or taking us to the Boy's Club or
some nursery, he'd do the way he did. It wasn't all that
bad. Sometimes it got cold or the television wouldn't
work or the food might spoil, but my brother and I had
each other, so for the most part we were all right.

One week our daddy got drunk and locked us in
the house without providing well-enough. After a
couple of days without Daddy, the cupboards got thin
and we started to worry. We lived off honey and mustard and peanut butter, and we ate all the cookies and
crackers we could find. But after a while it just wasn't
enough.

Our daddy'd usually never left us for more than a
day, but there we were, going on a week, with nothing
to do but stare at the television or watch the darkness
cover over the day through the window. My brother
said there were all kinds of ways we could escape: climb
through a window, break down a door, phone the
neighbors for help. But it was kind of an adventure trying not to starve to death, so we held out for Daddy.

One day I was particularly stir crazy and running a
fever, supposedly. I went to my brother out of my head
and told him if I died he could eat me to live on. It was
something I'd seen on TV. He said it was the very least I
could do, seeing that I'd eaten most of his food anyway,
and that if I died he wouldn't hesitate to take me up on
the offer. But after a long night of neardeath I got better
and he took to my sickness. He lay curled up on the
living room rug, ribs like bikespokes poking through
his undershirt, a bottle of medicine tucked beneath his

body and a tattered quilttop keeping out the cold. Because I was sure he was a goner, I asked him if I could eat him if he died. He said I could, but he'd barely make a morsel. He said he tasted like liver and onions; he doubted I could get him down without gagging any.

It was about the middle of the seventh day our daddy'd left us that my brother started to spit up blood. I brought him pillows and turned down the television and sat beside him. Outside we heard kids playing in the street and airplanes overhead and slamming doors; it wasn't so lonesome hearing folks move about. After some time I asked my brother if I could do anything, but he didn't answer. I could see then that he wasn't breathing, and I took a dining room chair and threw it through the sliding glass door and ran to the neighbors for help. They called an ambulance, and the lady of the house, a skinny black woman who smelled like creamed corn, cleaned me up and fixed me food and gave me a nice bed to sleep in. I thought my brother'd died, and I didn't see him again for a while.

My Daddy came back home after two weeks' absence, and the neighbors told him where I was. He came shouting at the black lady, who locked her door and called the police and had her two brothers help take Daddy in. He stayed in jail for about a month, and when he returned home he had my brother with him. Both were thin and desperate looking, whereas I was altogether cornfed. I asked my brother where he'd been.

"First," he said, "after I died, I went to the hospital, intensive care unit. When I got well they put me in a state house and I messed around with the kids there. Then Daddy come and got me."

I was sort of sad-feeling when I said goodbye to the black lady—she'd treated me so white and everything—but the first night back with our daddy made the homecoming worthwhile. He bought us pizza and Coca-Cola, and told us not to tell Mama what had happened when she came home for Christmas, and promised us he'd never leave us alone so long again. After he'd gone to sleep that night my brother roused me from bed and took me to the spot on the living room floor where he'd said he'd died—and I didn't doubt him any because I was the one who'd seen him not breathing. I'd been there for the whole blood-spitting thing.

"You want to know what death's like?"

I told him I did.

"Good. Because if you know what it's like, then you can't be scared of it. You are scared of it, aren't you?"

I told him I supposed I was, but how could anyone be scared of anything if they didn't have any idea what it was like?

"That's the whole dilemma," my brother said. "People got to see something to be afraid of it. Well, I've seen it. And I'm telling you there ain't nothing to be scared of."

But I told him that still didn't make any sense—he could describe a sasquatch or a pitbull to me, and I'd be pretty awful scared if I hadn't known what one was before.

He just looked at me. "You want to know what death is like or not?"

I told him I did.

"All right."

He sat on the floor, Seminole-style. I could tell it was going to be a lot of baloney, but I owed it to him to give it a listen.

"Death," he began, "has a million hands. Each holds something. Up comes the darkness and you see a cup of blood. Down comes the darkness and you see a stretch of street. You're lying awake, right? You feel your blood ebb. And the light draws from you and your heart folds over and on comes the darkness and then you see the hands. They're something, really. Words can't tell how many. But one holds a baby and the other holds a dying man; one holds your mother and the other holds your father; and some you kiss and some you spit on, and some you bite and some you hold; and some try to grab you, but you tear yourself away, and some open up and you feel yourself fall through. But I've seen them all, and each holds something. One shit, another dirt; one water, another food. We could sit here forever, couldn't number them all. We could separate all of the things in the world—wouldn't never have enough to fill up the hands of death."

He was quiet then, and we heard the world around us; I felt like I was squatting in the navel of everything. After a good ten minutes he told me to shut my eyes.

"Hear it?" he said.

I wasn't sure I could. There were cars, and dogs, and sirens, and crickets, but I couldn't hear death, I couldn't hear it anywhere. I wanted to hear it—it seemed so important—but in the end I confessed I couldn't.

"That's right," he told me. "That's goddamn right. Now close your eyes again, and I'll show you what death is."

I must have passed the better part of an hour waiting to be shown. And though I could smell the night through the open window, and feel the darkness like sackcloth against my eyelids, and hear the steady sound of my brother's breathing, I didn't know what he meant until his hand fell on my shoulder.

So when he curled himself up in a lump on the street and started to moan like he'd done so many times, I knew to leave him alone. There wasn't no one that could help him. He was staving off the hands.

He rose from the street after having settled down and did not look at me as he walked past me to the frontyard of the house where our mama lived.

"How do you get to the backyard?" he asked me.

I told him I could show him.

"Don't show me," he said. "Just go there."

"But it's a ditch," I said. "You want me to wait in a ditch?"

"That's right," he said. "Wait in the ditchwater."

I looked at him.

"Are you going to talk to Mama?"

"I'm going to see her."

"Are you going to talk to her?"

He did not so much look at me as through me.

"Wait in the water of the ditch," he said. "I am going to see her."

I did not tell him I would wait for him, and I did not tell him that I wouldn't. I walked away without saying anything. When I was sure he thought I'd gone, I crouched behind a fullspread ligustrum and watched him from where he couldn't see me.

He stood in the gutter before the frontyard, not moving or seeming to want to. The streetlight lit him from top to bottom, and his skin, what you could see of it beneath the blood, looked like somebody'd gone over it with a yellow paint roller. His eyes were opened wide and filled with that look, and a cigarette hung uncoiling on his lip. He took in the face of the house like a wrestler takes in the face of an opponent. He must not have moved for the better part of ten minutes, and I didn't know how long I could watch him and keep from falling asleep.

Above me, at the side window where my mama was sleeping, I heard Bohannon snoring. It sounded like a herd of cattle stampeding or a convoy of diesel trucks or a loud-ringing pneumatic drill or a thirteen-story building collapsing. I couldn't understand how my mama could bring herself to sleep with a calamity such as that, and I rose up quiet to peek through the bedroom window, but the ledge was too high for me to see over. I imagined if I'd been taller I could've seen Bohannon lying beneath the bedcovers with his mouth open wide enough for a body to fish bass in, and my mama on her side, her head propped up on her arm, wondering how she ever let herself get fixed in such a situation. But I knew more than likely that wouldn't be the case, whether for real or in my imagination. Bohannon was pretty much the only boy for Mama. Had I been able to look up over the window ledge I probably would've seen the two of them wrapped in one another's arms like the day I came home from school and found them together—and she'd probably have her whole entire ear up at Bohannon's mouth, taking in that racket like it were some sort of lullaby.

It made me uneasy to be beneath the same window where those two were lying, though I supposed I should've been used to it by then. For the most part I was immune to the company my mama'd kept; but with Bohannon it was less like company, more like she'd left my daddy and gotten remarried altogether. It didn't bother me none, though. Some things you can't do diddly about.

The day my mama left she never told none of us what it was she was doing. She just did it.

It was a Friday, the day she'd come back from the clinic with her face looking like a forced-together jigsaw puzzle. She went into the Florida room where our daddy was half out of his head, and she said a bunch of things that were too fast for me to follow. When she finished with him Daddy let out a wail like somebody'd put a spade through the mound of his belly and worked it clear through on up to his heart. I remembered how he rose himself up off the davenport and took a wild roundhouse at her, and how she pulled that can of something from her pocketbook and gave him a big old spray in the nose. He toppled back on the sofa hollering and clawing at his eyes, and my brother and me looked hard at our mama. We were proud of her; if anyone had had it coming, it had been our daddy.

He used to come home from work late at night, stumbling and pushing things over, telling everybody about the sonsofbitches, and how the sonsofbitches had done this or that to him, and how the sonsofbitches were plotting his ruination, and how the world was nothing but a sonsofbitches shitpile and no decent hard-working guy could ever get an even break. Mama, who worked herself, would give him his supper re-

gardless of his mood, and he'd throw it against the wall
or taste it and spit the whole thing out or make a face
maybe and pound his fists in the manner of a bad-
behaved kindergartner. Mama took it like a concrete
pillar, without so much as a mean look, cross word, or
inch of self-pity. But after a while I supposed she
couldn't take it anymore, so she left.

We'd helped her pack. While Daddy was in the
Florida room digging at his eyes we helped her get
things together in the bedroom. "Get me this," she
would tell us. "Fetch me that over there." We didn't ask
her where she was going nor why she was going there
nor when she'd return. It wasn't any of our business.
When all her stuff was packed and ready, she bent
down and squeezed my brother so hard I heard a rib
crack. She took me and held me out at arm's length and
looked me long in the face; that is, we looked each other
long in the face. In her, I could see from where I'd come.
She was awfully beautiful and had the kind of eyes that
made you feel like you were falling backwards into
water.

Above me, through the window, Bohannon's snoring stopped. I heard him turn his body in bed and mur-
mur to himself in his sleep: "All right. I got it. It's in my
hand. It's notarized." He spoke quickly, and loud, and
his voice had a pitiful, panicky tone to it, like someone
who's had something loved stolen permanently away
from him. "All right. Attaboy. You can trust me, son.
Attaboy." I wondered what he was dreaming about, or
whether he dreamed at all; wondering whether Bohannon dreamed was like wondering whether a dog did—
it was sort of unsettling just thinking about it. "What?
How's that? Come back here! It's me, boy, it's me! Oh,

you don't . . . you just don't get it!" Whatever type of dream it was, it certainly must have been something, 'cause soon enough I heard Bohannon weeping. But, like a quick-leaking faucet, Bohannon put an end to the waterworks in no time, and got back to his infernal snoring.

I crouched low behind the ligustrum and looked out again at my brother. He stood in the gutter like a puppet with an armful of string, and his face had a flushed, exhausted look to it. He had another cigarette in his mouth, though this one weren't nothing but a stub, and I noticed that every couple of minutes or so his left hand would work itself into a regular spasm. Gas from the can in his nervous hand sloshed onto my brother's fingers, and the fuel caused the blood to peel itself away; there were long streaks of raw skin showing in the yellow streetlight. I imagined if I had a mind to, I could've peeled my brother right down to the bone. The gasoline seemed to wash him clean through.

Now the death of the night had just begun, and the burnt-out, copper-colored glow of the morning was beginning to come on. It was pitch dark, mind you, but a lighter pitch than the previous hour, and you could tell it was going to get gradually lighter. The streetlamps kicked suddenly on to a less powerful glow, and I could see my brother, however faintly, eyeing the house from the downslope of the gutter. In the distance, a closetful of thunder slid open, rolling like bowling balls across the heavy sky. My brother looked up, closed his eyes, and stepped from the gutter. He threw down his cigarette and crossed Bohannon's lawn, dousing the grass with gasoline. When he came to a tree he'd douse it too, pouring a palmful in his hand and smearing it slowly on the trunk's puffed belly. He went to Bohannon's milktruck and covered the hood with gasoline, then he did all the plants in the frontporch flower box, and the lawnchairs, and the screen on the frontdoor.

He wanted to climb onto the roof, so he stuck the can of gasoline beneath his underarm, reached up for the trellis, and began to scramble up the ironwork. When he'd reached the roof I moved from my hiding place out onto the street to get a better view of him. I bent down behind a punched-up Chrysler Plymouth and watched his shadow play across the pointed roof of Bohannon's house. He crouched down on his knees, squash-bodied like a spider, and tipped the spout of the gas can to the gutters and blacktar rooftiles. When he came to a spot below a window he'd spread himself out belly down on the tar and shake the can hard backwards, so whatever gas flew out of the can drenched the glass of the windows.

He disappeared for a moment, and I supposed he'd gone to do the chimney and weathervane. Only when he came back did I appreciate what a thorough job he'd done. The roof seemed to glisten with a fresh sweat, and the wind carried the beautiful stench of the gasoline to you. All in all, he'd covered the whole house pretty good. He even had gas enough to douse the bushes in the planters.

To check his work, my brother walked the length of the roof four times, making absolutely sure he hadn't missed a spot. When he'd finished he set the gasoline at his feet and moved his right arm one way, like when you drive in a nickel nail, and his left arm the other, like when you saw dead wood. He took off his jacket and undershirt and bent down and picked up the can of gasoline. Tilting the spout, he doused his neck and face and hair and chest. His entire body shone with whatever fuel remained.

He reached for the pack of matches in his pocket and I called out his name and ran to him.

"Hey!"

He didn't answer me.

"Hey! Hey! What're you doing there?"

He was trying to strike a match, but the length of his body was shaking so hard he couldn't manage it.

"Hey!" I said his name again. "What's that you're doing? What's that you got there?" I looked at the unlit matches in his hands. "You want me to go and do that now? You want me to light one for you?"

His body froze. The hand that held the box of matches fell to his side, and he swallowed hard and stared down at me. He had an angry, ashamed, lost look on his face. When he spoke his voice crept out in a hoarse whisper, like his words were pieces of ice thawing.

"What did you say?"

"I said do you want me to light that match for you?"

He looked at me harder, swallowing and figuring, then squatted down like a baseball catcher and gave me the once-over.

"Did you say you'd light the match for me?"

"That's what I said."

"I don't want to smoke a cigarette, you know."

"I know," I told him. "I know what you want to do."

He snorted.

"Oh, do you?"

"Uh-huh."

He scratched his head.

"I bet you do. I bet you goddamn do."

I held out my hand toward him, so he could throw the matches to me.

"Nuh-uh," he said. "You gotta come up here."

I looked at the roof, and I looked at him on it. I didn't think he would make me do that; I didn't think he was so far gone as to ask that of me.

"You want me to light it up there?"

He nodded and laughed.

"That's right. That's what I want. You afraid?"

I looked at the ground.

"I ain't afraid."

"You like to play with fire?"

I looked up from the ground.

"I ain't afraid."

"Then you come on up. You come up here, and I tell you what—you won't come down."

"I told you twice I ain't afraid."

"Then you come on and show me," he said. He held out the matches where I couldn't reach them. "You just come on up."

I went to the trellis and climbed it. On the roof of Bohannon's house I saw the whole city laid out in a jigsaw of alleys and houses. It made me dizzy to be up there and I could barely make my legs work. I got to my brother and he rubbed his hands across his cheek and neck and smeared my face and hair with the gasoline. The cuts from where he'd hit me before stung from the fuel and I drew a quick breath and panted like a dog locked in a hot car. My brother looked at me and smiled, smiled through the blood and gas and yellow skin. "Hurts, don't it?" he said. "Hurts like the living hell." With a swing of his arm he indicated the city around us. "You know what I wish? I wish we had a can big enough to do the town. That's what I wish. If we did, I'd be able to light the match myself. If it were the world, well, you'd better believe I could." He sat himself down on the roof. "What did you think I had this gasoline for?"

I looked at the empty can.

"I knew why you had it."

"You say that now."

"No," I told him. "I knew. I knew long before, back when you were in the shed."

He scraped his knuckles against the tiles of the roof. "You knew," he said. "You know goddamn everything."

I turned my back to him, took in the city.

In Bohannon's backyard blackbirds had gathered single file on a wire. They were meaner than hell, and kept trying to push one another off. I wondered why they didn't get electrocuted, bouncing on and off the wire the way they did. It was something my brother would know. He was a nut for things like that, a regular authority. I said his name.

"Stop saying that."

"How come?"

"Because I don't want to hear it."

His chest was working up and down like our daddy's would after medicine, and he clung to the corner of the roof like an animal. I did not turn my look away from him.

"You give me the matches."

He did not answer.

"You give me the matches," I repeated. I said his name.

"I told you not to—"

"Give me the matches."

"—say my name."

"I knew why you had the gasoline."

"You say that."

"I knew when you were doing tricks at the drive-in."

"You—"

"I knew when the night fell you didn't need gasoline; I knew when the day broke you'd manage it with anything."

"—say that."

"Now give me the matches, like you said."

"I ain't—"

"You thought I was afraid."

"—gonna—"

"Afraid of it."

"—give 'em."

"But I ain't like you. I ain't like you and I ain't like her and I ain't like Daddy and I ain't like anyone. I ain't afraid of what's got to be done. Now give me those—"

He reached between his legs and handed me the matches. He did not throw them at me, he handed them.

"Here," he said. "Here."

We were breathing like horses. Our eyes were in each other's.

"Listen," I said, as if I needed to tell him, "I ain't afraid of it."

I walked to the edge of the roof and struck the match. For a moment I stared into the mouth of the flame, then I dropped it in the planter. The bushes caught fire, and the grass did. Then the house went; I could smell it burning.

"Jesus!" my brother said. He had my head beneath his arm, and we were running up the roof, down the roof. "Jesus!" he said. "Jesus!" And it was the strangest thing, all of it, and though I kept turning it around, I couldn't figure it out.

We squatted in the water of the ditch and watched it die. I knew I was out of my head, but as I stared at the fire I imagined I could see a flower becoming stalk and a stalk becoming flower. I supposed it was the kind of thing you could think better than describe, but it was like there was a magnolia blossom before my eyes, and an invisible hand would come along and pick it clean, then up from the stalk would rise a new ring of petals, and so forth and so on. After a while I couldn't even see the burning anymore. I just saw a big wall of white-hot blossoms and a field of moving hands, and the whole scene was forever dying and undying before me.

My brother knelt next to me in the water, but he wasn't watching the house burn. You'd think he would've been, but he wasn't. He had his face down in the water, and he looked like a drowning man whose feet still clung to the floor of the ocean. Every once in a while he lifted his face from the surface of the ditch-water and blew a spout of steam in the smoking air, then his throat would gulp and gulp and he'd plunge his head back down into the water. The way he was doing, he missed everything. He didn't even see the woman.

She came into the backyard with a wet dishrag across her face and a baseball bat in her right hand. A little girl in a patched-up nightgown followed her hollering and coughing. "Is the backdoor like the frontdoor?" she cried. "Is it locked on the inside like the front is, Mama?" When the woman heard the little girl's voice, she ran to her. She took the hem of the little girl's nightgown and showed her how to hold it up over her face so she wouldn't inhale any of the smoke. The little girl did how she'd been told and stood in the farthest corner of the backyard, away from the smoke. Beneath her gown she was naked.

The woman left the girl and ran to the backporch of the burning house. She swung the bat through the sliding glass door, and smoke billowed up from the mouth of the fire. The woman stumbled backwards, like somebody'd struck her in the jaw, then she shook herself to her senses and ran groping for the little girl. In the darkness of the smoke the girl wasn't even looking for her mother. She merely trembled and hollered in all the commotion, and when her mother found her she lifted her quickly and the little girl's gown tore away from her body. You could see the whiteness of her skin beneath the swimming thick smoke, and it gave the impression that the little girl had never bathed, not even once.

The firemen arrived too late, looking like a bunch of lost football players. They carried their hose like a glutted pet snake and turned the nozzle on huddled pieces of slow-burning furniture. There wasn't much left of the house.

I could hear the voices of neighbors and other people standing in the street in front of the house. From all the noises of cardoors slamming, I could tell a lot of people had gathered. The air was practically shoe-polish black from the smoke of the fire, and I imagined the faces of the neighbors would be smudged like the faces of cannibals and chimney sweeps. I imagined their eyes would be hard too, like marbles. A fire, like a mirror, was something to see and see into.

It was early morning, or at least it was supposed to be. The air was humid and close-fitting, like a wet shirt, and gray light hung low on the edge of the horizon. We felt like we were trapped in the stomach of an animal, like a thing just eaten or about to be spit out, and the sun, which barely showed itself, looked like a curious outraged eye staring inside-out at the thing it had swallowed.

I'd taken a lot of smoke, and my brother had to carry me from the ditch. I wasn't much with myself, but I remembered him lifting me and dipping me in the ditch-water once to wash all the darkness off of me. I also remembered him carrying me at a slant down the slope of the ditch for the better part of forever, the noises of the sirens and cars and people dwindling down to the sounds of my chest water-whistling. When he laid me down on the ground the earth seemed to rush up beneath me like a roof caving in backwards, and I knew that I could hear, barely, and see, somewhat, and he stood above me sort of crooked-leaning.

"You all right?"

He said it, leaning, me barely able to see.

"I didn't— Wait. Let me say it." He had his hand up around his mouth; he kept taking it off and putting it back on, like fingers around a shook-up pop bottle. "Wait. Wait. Let me say it, now. I didn't—I didn't see her. Wait. Let me say it. Nobody got out."

It could have been his crying then, if only it had been crying. It could have been his laughter, maybe, but it was more than that. It was a sound unlike anything I'd heard—unlike laughter or crying or music or language. It was the type of sound that rises from the throat like pressure that can't be stopped, like a water-pumped rocket toy or a coffee kettle or an oil geyser, and my brother kept putting his fingers to his mouth, pulling them away, putting them back—and when he spoke, his words strung together in a whistle, and he didn't take no pause between sentences like folks you see at public libraries who ought to be removed, who ought to be put away.

"Listen," he said, that noise gushing out: "When. When they see him. Wait. Ha, ha. Just let me. Ha, ha. Just let me say it. When. When they see him there—" Hands up around his mouth, fumbling, a muzzle on the mouth of a rabid animal: "When they see him there. On the floor, there. They'll think—" Whistling: "They'll think he did it!"

My eyes were open then, but I wanted to close them. I knew I couldn't. I lay there, quiet, just staring at that mouth like you might stare into a wound or the hole of a toilet, not listening to the noise that was beyond tears or laughter, not listening to that noise like choking and being choked and wanting to scream but not being able to, not listening to the whistle, or watching the way his fingers fumbled with his lips, ten soft corks and an unstopped bottle. And how, in the end, when his shaking had stopped, I decided it was closer to laughter, how if it was closest to anything, it was closest in the end to laughter.

"It's just us"—whistling—"just me and you"— heaving now—"just the two of us"—choking on it— "and nobody else." So it was all right if he screamed, it was all right if he let the pressure out once, because when he was through he seemed a good deal calmer, and he did not sweat as much nor put his hands up to his mouth, and I did not have to listen to his teeth talking to themselves: "Can you believe it! Oh Christ, can you believe it!"

It was light, and we had begun to walk. There was not as much blood on my brother, what from the water of the ditch and all.

"We can't keep on like this."

One of us said it, it didn't matter who.

"I don't see how we can keep on like this."

My eyes were with the ground, watching it come up, fall back, come up, fall back. It made me sick to look at it.

"We haven't eaten."

"Yes we have."

I kept my eyes on the ground, getting sick.

"Sometimes you've eaten but you just can't remember."

"A lot of people haven't eaten, but we have."

"When? I can't remember when."

My stomach felt like a bag of sour water. Every once in a while it made a wounded sound, like it was leaking inside of me.

"You hungry?"

"I am."

"No you ain't. You just sound it."

I wasn't watching my brother no more. Even if I looked at him I couldn't see him. It was as if there was something between the two of us, a body you couldn't get through or around. The only way I knew he was there was by the sound of his voice, which didn't sound like him anyway. For all I knew there might have been a complete stranger walking in front of me, and at that point it wouldn't have mattered, at that point he wasn't even there.

"Hey?"

He turned around and looked at me.

"What is it?"

"I." I was trying to think of it, what it was I'd meant to tell him. "Listen." His face, it wasn't nothing but a face to me. I put my hand up to it, but it passed right through. "Listen. I'm not sure what. Tell me who you are, there. Tell me who you are."

He got down on his knees and looked at me, but I didn't see him. He told me.

"I don't believe you."

"No. Neither do I."

He stood back up and walked beyond me, back in the direction from where we came. I asked him where he was going.

"To the ditch."

"Again? But we just—"

"I know. I can't walk no more. I got to float. If somebody sees me like this they'll call the police. I can't go around walking like this no more. You come with me, all right?"

He knew I'd follow him; he didn't have to ask. All I wanted to know was where we were heading.

"I ain't sure." We were at the slope of the ditch. "You ain't going to drown on me, now?"

I told him no, I was tall enough. Besides, it was only a sewage ditch.

"I don't know if we're dressed right for a sewage ditch," he said. "I just don't know." He held out his hands at his sides. "You think I'm dressed all right for a sewage ditch?"

I looked at him. There was less blood on him from the first time we'd been in the ditch. I told him.

"Less blood on me. Well. I swallowed a lot of ditchwater before. Must've swallowed my share of blood too. Have you got that taste in your mouth?"

I didn't know what taste he meant, so I didn't answer him. We were wading down the sewage canal, wading through the warmth of the teabrown water. It felt like a warm bath, like a good warm Sunday bath.

"Did you hear me?"

"What?"

"Don't fall asleep on me now. You fall asleep and the ditchwitch'll get you. Only sonsofbitches let the ditchwitch getcha. I said you got that taste in your mouth? Do you got it?"

"What taste?" I dunked my face in the ditch and

swallowed some of the water. "You mean that taste? You mean the taste of ditchwater?"

"No, no. You wanna catch bowel cancer? What I meant was the blood taste. You know. Like when you suck on a penny. Like when you put a copper penny on your tongue and let it sit there. You got that taste?"

I dipped my face in the ditch again.

"Stop that."

"All right."

"And answer my question."

"About what? About the blood taste?"

He nodded his head.

"Right. Uh-huh. You got it?"

I said I did, and when I went to dunk my head a third time to drink he pulled me up by the neck and slapped me in the face.

"Don't do that anymore."

"I won't. I promise. I got the taste."

He let go of me.

"You told me already."

I looked at him.

"I told you?"

"Uh-huh."

We came to the part of the ditch that branched out in a fork to the old part of the bay. I touched the place on my face where my brother had slapped me, then I turned to him.

"You know," I said. "I can't see you. I can't make out your face, or your voice, or who you are. You could be a haunt for all I know."

My brother shook his head.

"Ha ha. You're just tired and hungry is all. We'll

get something in you and your head'll clear up. You want me to get you something for your head?"

"But I've got the taste."

He studied his feet.

"I know that. I know you do. You want I should get you something that will take the taste away?"

I stared at him. Through the dimming night I could make out his features a little more clearly. There was a busted smile on the right side of his face, like somebody'd been tugging too hard on his upper lip, and the lids of his eyes twitched and squinched and fluttered. His face was washed clothesline white in the water of the ditch, and tiny flecks of dirt and crud had collected in his hair.

"You want I should get you something?"

His voice was coming to itself, too, like somebody with their hand on a radio dial bringing the tuner gradually onto the right station. I said his name and felt the world draw away from me. I was under the water, and I could feel his arms grabbing.

"Come on! Jesus Christ!"

I was out of the water and my eyes were sort of rolling and the whole world looked something like the fabric of an unfolded shirt. My brother was talking to me.

"You fainted. That's all. You only fainted. Now breathe deep." I did it. "That's right," he told me.

We were coming up on a bridge that separated the canal from the old bay. I wasn't so much moving anymore as my brother was holding me and I was moving with him. There was a trim old black man on the bridge eating something from a Campbell's soup can, and when he saw us he put the can down and hitched his trousers and shouted.

"You boys! You there! 'M'on out of that water!"

My brother and I didn't answer him, and the black man put his hands up around his mouth.

"I say you there! Playin' Dead Man's Float! You can't be passing under this hyah bridge—I got my traps on the other side!"

The old man's voice was pretty loud, so I could tell he was right above us. We passed beneath the belly of the bridge and into the cool and the damp of the hollow. There was a sound of water dripping, and the echo of my own breathing came at me from all sides, and I could see our shadows moving on the far wall of the bridge supporters like hands in a shadow play. We came back into the grayness of the morning and saw the black man with his head between his hands, tromping up and down and spitting into the water. He talked to the sky, as if it were the only thing that would listen to him, and he shook his fist at the water, as if it were to blame. "People do as they do," he said. "People do as they do. You say watch out. You say looky here. Ain't nothin' but deafmutes, blindmen, motherfo's, and monkeysees. And look at these tomcats, comin' on through. Ribber rats! Homeboys! People do as they do!"

When my brother and I were a good ways from the bridge—in a deeper, swifter part of the canal where the sewage had ended and the old bay began—we pulled ourselves onto a low-tide sandbar and sat looking at the canal trailing in a thread behind us. I could see the old man moving back and forth on the narrow bridge, and I could hear that he was still shouting but had a hard time figuring out exactly what he was saying. I turned to look at my brother and noticed a wooden trap full of moving bluecrabs sitting in the water at his side.

There was a piece of cut rope tied to the top of the trap, and the knife glinted in my brother's pants pocket.

"We're going to sell these crabs and get something for your head," my brother told me.

"I don't need anything," I said. "I feel all right."

"We got eight dollars' worth of bluecrab here."

"You buy yourself some medicine," I told him.

I watched the bluecrabs struggle in the cage. They made a funny, brutal noise, like football shoulder pads clicking together.

"I wasn't going to buy it for myself. I was going to buy it for you."

"Well," I said. "I don't need it."

He stuck his finger into the trap, and a crab latched on to it. It didn't seem to hurt him much.

"You passed out back there," he said. "You were out of your head." He loosed his finger from the crab's clutches. "You know what I think?"

I didn't know.

"What I think is you're still out of your head."

I looked at him.

"You're the one with your hand in the crabtrap."

All told, three different crabs had latched on to my brother's fingers. It made him smile.

"But they don't hurt none," he said. "They only hurt a little."

He stood and picked the trap up by its string.

"You want me to sell this for money?"

I did not answer him.

"Eight dollars," he said. "We could get things."

I put my hands in the water and lifted some to my face.

"All right," my brother said. "All right, I hear you."

He began to walk and I did not follow him. I watched him wade back into the current and saw him disappear in the direction of the bridge where the black man was cursing the sky and the water. For a while his head disappeared beneath the tide, and I knew he was tying the crabtrap to the old fishing rope. When he came out from under the water I could see the black man shaking his fist and hoisting his trousers and spitting at him. Because it did not take my brother long to swim to where he'd left me waiting, I knew he was all right again. And because he was all right I knew he would need more medicine. It was always the way.

"I give him back his crabs," he said.

"Yes," I told him. "I saw it."

After resting awhile in the water we reached the shore and started walking toward the part of the old bay where the abandoned city ports and railway yards were. I wasn't thinking about the crabs anymore, but my brother punched me in the shoulder once and looked at me and then down at the sand.

"I don't need a bunch of goddamn crabs to get a bottle of medicine when I want one."

"I know it," I said; there wasn't any sense in arguing.

Some time passed, and we hadn't said anything. I looked at my brother and told him that I thought it was going to rain again.

He opened his mouth and tasted the air.

"Yes," he said. "I think you're right."

We crossed a stretch of sand and sea oats that led to the old bay shipping yards. As my brother walked ahead of me across the squatting dunes, he gathered oats in a bundle beneath his underarm. It was illegal to pick them, and my brother knew it. He did not have to be able to read to know what he was doing was considered wrong. You could get anywhere from thirty to ninety days in jail, plus a one-thousand-dollar fine, just for picking one oat from the side of a sand dune, but my brother didn't care. He must have had a good two dozen in his arms when he came to the lip of the old bay harbor, and as he stared out at the shipyards, which were quiet and lifeless as the marina we'd hidden in the night before, he took each of the oats and tossed them reed by reed into the stillwater of the dead bay.

"Look at her," he said, eyes practically beneath the water. "Will you just look?"

Time was, or so our mama'd told us, that the old bay ports were the busiest in the area. In the night, you could hear ships calling to the lights of the harbor city, and folks would gather in bars by the port to drink and talk in different tongues and open each other up with bowie knives. But now the port lay like a fish left to spoil, the whole place reeking of salt and rusted iron, the wreck of a spongeboat sideways tilted in the gray gritted teeth of a sharp coral reef.

On one of the barges, across the harbor, I saw two girls playing Hide-and-Go-Seek. One of the girls was older than the other, and she lay resting her head against a pile of ancient-looking chains. The younger, meanwhile, hid huddled behind a heap of brokendown crates and boxes. I wasn't sure how they'd gotten onto the barge, or why they'd wanted to get there in the first place, but I watched them chasing each other and wished that I were there with them.

The stomach of the sky had grown bigger and darker and the wind had a full wet flavor to it. I knew the next storm was bound to be terrific. My brother was headed in the direction of the old bay bridge, which stretched across the harbor a good quarter mile and led from the train tracks back into the city. The bridge wasn't open to traffic anymore, but folks who wanted to fish off of it could pull their trucks or station wagons onto it. From where I was I could see a lot of morning people out there on the bridge. It made my brother nervous, I knew, because wherever a lot of folks gathered there was bound to be a cop around to keep them in line, and wherever there was a cop was where my brother didn't want to be.

We were both soaking wet and must have looked like the resurrected drowned, but my brother kept his mouth shut and took to the bridge with the confidence of the man who might've owned it. It was tough making out the faces of the people who were fishing, the air was so ashen from the suffering sky, but what few eyes regarded us stared out in dull red pinpoints of light, and occasionally a ladyfinger of lightning would reveal a face full of weary anger and disinterest. In weather such as that it might as well have been night, and the men and women of the bridge wandered about and talked to each other in a scattered, helpless way, like dogs that have a hunch they're about to be beaten but don't have anywhere to run to and don't have any way in which to fight back. So the people gathered in miserable company.

It was the kind of rev-up for a storm that made your chest pound with dread and anticipation, and though many of the families had left in their cars, all those that stayed had gathered side by side at the railing of the bridge to look at the water and study the sky. There were women in halter tops and kimonos and bikini bottoms standing like teapots with their hands on their hips, and men in bluejeans, not wearing any shirts, hunched around their fishing poles half-awake from fear and weariness. A couple little kids stood beneath the arms and legs of their parents, swinging from their mama's hips or rotating about their daddy's knees, but the parents didn't pay them much mind. Once in a while they'd reach back a hand and stroke the little kid's face or hair, but otherwise they kept their eyes keen on the sky and water, as if the storm might break the instant they looked away, as if they might miss at the one moment least worthy of looking away the one moment most worth waiting for.

In the distance I could hear a train in the railway yards beyond the port. Sure enough, a white pillar of smoke moved like a huge bird across the dark sky, and beneath it I could see the chain of heavy swaying cars as the train pulled slowly through the city. When at first I saw the smoke I imagined it was from Bohannon's house, but I knew the smoke from the fire had been black, and only white smoke like that from a train would show itself moving in a storm-eaten sky. Black swallowed black in the case of a storm, in the case of smoke or fire in a bad-weather sky.

"After the storm," my brother said, "whenever it comes, you'll see morning full. It wasn't dark like this thirty minutes ago. Oh, it was dark all right, it was night even, but it wasn't dark like this. After the storm breaks it'll rain hard and fast, then, when the worst is done, it'll drizzle for an hour or two. It'll be drizzling in full daylight, and you won't remember none of this."

We were almost off the bridge and beyond all the people, and there wasn't any sign of a cop anywhere. Quickly, then, as if he scented something, my brother stopped and turned and walked to the railing of the old bay bridge. I went up beside him, and we looked out across the bay. I watched where his finger was pointing.

Over the water, no more than a halfmile out, the air hung gray-speckled from a quick summer squall, and beyond that, about two miles off in the east, a long whitish-charcoal thing, shaped like an upside-down cornucopia, hovered above the waterline.

"Funnel cloud," I whispered.

My brother nodded.

"Waterspouts," he said.

He pointed again to the vicinity of where I was looking, then his hand began to scan farther to the east.

"You see that?" he asked me.

"The funnel cloud?" I said.

He brought his hand down. "Uh-huh," he answered. "All three of 'em."

I looked harder, right where his hand had pointed, and saw them. Floating, cone-shaped, like suspension ladders extended from earth to heaven, the other two stood there, hovering in the background of the first and largest waterspout. Altogether they looked like panty hose hung up on a shower rod, or skinny barracuda on a fishmarket scale, and they meant that we might have tornadoes inland, that the fishermen and their families camped out on the old bay bridge might get hit by three brewing cyclones.

"Do you think they see them?" I asked my brother.

He turned to look at the people, then we were walking again.

"Hunh," he said. "It's all they can see. Those folks is hypnotized, look at them. They can't take their eyes off of it. Sometimes you've got to have strength to look away."

We passed the barge where the little girls were playing. I noticed then that one of them was not so little, that, in fact, she wasn't even a girl. She was a woman, old enough to be pregnant, and she rested her head against the same chain pile, holding her swollen stomach and laughing at the sky. I could tell she was having a good time. I didn't have to ask her.

Spray from the dead barge blew across us over the water as we passed through the last of the deserted port. As I walked away from the pitching barge I could hear the laughter of the pregnant girl growing. I'd never heard a woman's voice—or anyone's for that matter—get gradually louder as you moved away from it. It was as if the wind were blowing it up with air, placing it like toy balloons beneath our tired feet; every step I took seemed to make the girl's voice break all the louder. Just when I thought we were out of her range I'd hear one last uncontrolled pop, and soon it'd be followed by another. After it had died out completely I realized it was a sound I wasn't likely to forget. Like a carnival calliope or a buzzer in a house of horror or the laughter of a fatman in a circus freakshow, her voice had a unique music to it, a stamp all its own, and when we'd passed

completely through the old bay shipyards I could still
hear her music calling after me, playing around in my
head like a radio song you can't shake off.

We turned down a dirt road that cars took to get to
the bridge, and it led us to a white pebble hill where you
could see the railroad switchyards. The deserted switch-
ing house was made of tumbledown wood, and the windows had been broken into. A boy and a girl, about my
brother's age, sat holding each other on a busted bench.
When they saw us they squinted their eyes and fell back
into what they were doing, all wrapped in one another
like lovebirds in a pet store cage.

We stumbled down the white pebble hill and took
to the maze of the railroad tracks. I went immediately to
the track that was still in use and put my hand against
the steel railing to feel how warm it was. I called to my
brother. He came over, slowly.

"Put your hand there."

"On the track?"

I said yes.

He did it, and when he felt how warm it was he
laid himself out completely on the track, his whole body
across it.

"This is where I wanna come," he said. "This is
where I wanna come lay when I die."

I spread myself out on the track opposite his.

"You wait here and you'll get your wish. Trains
come on time every twenty-five minutes."

He stretched his arms out behind his head and
picked up a handful of pebbles. He threw them up into
the air, and some of them landed on his face and body.
He laughed.

"Then I better not stick around here," he said. "No, sir. I'd better goddamn not."

He sat up and turned and looked in the direction from where the next train would come.

"You see it?"

"No."

"I do," he said. "It's got a black face and white hollow eyes. It says its all right for me to be on the track, but you better get the hell off."

He looked at me.

"You know why?" he asked.

"No."

He didn't look at me no more.

"You know why."

I got up and started to walk. This time, he followed me.

We walked down the railroad tracks for less than a quarter-mile balancing like gymnasts on the balls of our feet. I ducked into the bushes to take a piss, and when I walked back up the white pebble hill I found him stretched out between the rails of the railroad tracks. His eyes were wide open, like an invisible hand was prying the lids, and the whole while he talked he wouldn't take his eyes off me.

"It's got a black face and white hollow eyes. It comes in the night when you're lying awake and says, 'Ohh. Ohh. Ohhhhhh!' Do you know what it is? I bet you do. Do you know what it is?"

I told him it was death.

"Ohh," he said, sort of speculative. "Ohh," in the same tone, but kind of amused. Then he wrapped his hands around his stomach and let out a ferocious bellow, almost as if there were something inside of him, something he had to push on to force out. "Ohhhhhh! Ohhhhhh!" Only when his eyes fell back into themselves and his legs straightened out did I realize he'd been laughing, that the answer I'd given his riddle amounted to one of the funniest things he had ever heard.

"Oh. Oh. Oh!" he shouted. "Death? Death? Is that what you said to me? I told you once, ain't you got any ears? I sat up on the tracks and said I seen it coming. Death? Goddamn it. That ain't the answer! It's a train, you idiot. What I meant was a train!"

I looked down the railroad track sort of southward and saw it, that thing with the black face and white hollow eyes, moving toward us at a comfortable crawl. It may have been death, I didn't know. But it looked like a train; it most certainly did. And it made the noise my brother'd described: "Ohh. Ohh. Ohhhhhh!"

"See?" he said. "See?" He had his back turned to me and was choking with laughter. His eyes were wild in the far-off lights of the train, and he had one hand on the knob of my shoulder trying to pull me down onto the tracks with him. "Do like me!" he hollered. "Do like me!"

"What do you mean, do like you?"

The train was still a good distance off, but it was getting closer by the minute; I could see the light.

"Do like me! Come on and do like me!"

I shoved his hand off of my shoulder.

"No, I ain't gonna do like you. Least not until I know what it is you want done."

"Listen," he said. He drew his breath. "It's easy. I

seen it in the movies. It's how you beat the trains. It's how you beat that big old monster. Look." He stopped grabbing at my shoulder and stretched out between the tracks as flat as a cedar two-by-four. "See? You lay low and it passes you over, like you ain't even there to be flattened, like you ain't even there to be seen. See?" He sat up quickly and lay flat again, to demonstrate. "You could lie next to me. The track's wide enough for two. It'll be a lot of fun. It'll show that you can beat it."

"Beat what?"

"The train! What do you think?"

He was grabbing at my shoulder again, trying to get me to lie down.

"You better hurry up," he told me. "This isn't any Saturday serial. This isn't any godforsaken to-be-continued deal. You've gotta make up your mind. I ain't gonna do it for you, and you haven't got a whole helluva lotta time to think."

Already my body was white from its glow. The cars weren't approaching at a breakneck pace, they were approaching sort of slow and thorough and self-assured, but I knew it wouldn't be long before they'd be upon us.

"Come on!" my brother said. "Stretch or be stretched. This isn't any goddamn grocery cart. This isn't the Sunday funnies and it isn't Truth or Dare. Stretch or be stretched."

I asked him if it'd be hot beneath the belly of the train.

"Ten times as hot as hell and twice as many devils shooting sparks up our asses."

I did not lie beside him, because I did not want to risk losing an arm, but I did place my feet sole to sole with his. I crossed my hands up over my face and took a huge gulp of stormbrewed air, as if I were preparing to spend a long time underwater. Then I heard my brother give a cowboy shout and the world became heat and steel and solid noise and I'd never hollered so loud or so long and nothing ever seemed so good or so true and I couldn't remember a time or a place when anything had felt so real, so satisfying.

Walk fast to your own end. I'll be there to see you. Go.

I rose with that flavor of my heart in my mouth and went to him. He was the color of clean bed linen and his body twitched like some darklived thing left to manage in the light. I dipped my hand in a railroad puddle and sprinkled his face with water.

"Over! What?" His eyes were not open. "It's almost what? It's almost over."

I sat beside him, waiting for his head to fall back together. I splashed his mouth with water while he babbled.

"What? Oh! I'm gonna live beneath the belly of a rolling bed of cottonmouthed firecrackers! I'm gonna stretch up these arms of steel and rattle the bars of the clattering cage! I've got a steamwhistle! I've got a grave-digger! I'm wide awake for the boneyard express!"

"Quiet."

I could see the train disappearing around the bend. It made less noise now that it was not above us.

"White eyes! What? What? White eyes of God the bluecrab!"

His arms were flung backward, fingers hooked around the ties as if the world, in complete disregard of the upside down and the undelivered, had suddenly decided to right itself.

I said it to him.

"What?"

I said it to him again.

"No. Oh, no." His eyes bobbed back pale and empty, showing veins. "Please. I can't. I already beat it once. You said it yourself. I don't have to beat it no more."

"That's right," I told him. "You already beat it once."

We could hear the train now.

"Ohh," it said. "Ohh. Ohhhhhh!"

I looked at him. He was coming to.

"I didn't make you. Remember that."

I wasn't sure if he could hear me.

"I didn't tell you that you had to do it."

He rolled over on his side curled up like a beebee pellet. His body looked like somebody was pulling on it, pulling from his feet.

"I want to go back," he said.

"We can't now."

I put the burlap sack beneath me and lay his down for him to sit on. The yellow plastic of the slide is warm from the nearness of the sun, and we can see the grounds of the school below us. There are kids behind us in line waiting to go down, and he just stands there, hands wadded into fists, not saying a word nor moving, not even looking as scared as he is.

"I had a dream about this once't," he says. "I climbed to the top of a carnival slide, and just as I was about ready to go

down, it started to come apart beneath me. I didn't die though. There was just that awful feeling of falling, and I knew it was a dream, but the falling wasn't any less horrible. I almost wished it weren't a dream so I could hit the earth and get myself killed and get all the falling over with."

He sets himself down on the burlap sack and we join hands as we fall. At the bottom of the slide he is all smiles and laughter and ready to pay another two quarters. I say, "I told you we couldn't climb down the steps we clumb up. Once you're at the top of a slide, you ain't got no option but to slide back down."

"Come on."

I helped him to his feet and we headed in the direction of the switchyard house. There was a half-blinking station light and behind it I could see those two mooneyed kids still feeling each other up like the world was coming to an end. I went to them and showed them the knife. They didn't run or anything, like I'd suspected, they just stopped what they were doing and sat there staring, almost as if they were closed in behind protective glass. They were both so young-looking I wouldn't have needed a knife to have hurt them. I wouldn't have needed nothing save my hands.

"Do you want us to git?" the girl said.

I nodded and sort of twisted the knife.

"That's right," I said. "That's what I want."

Her boyfriend sat there like a bump on a log, not even looking at me really, but taking me in sort of indirectly, as if my head were off center.

"We heard tell about the West Port strangler," said the boy. "You ain't him, are ya?"

I told him I wasn't and the girl started laughing.

"Oh, you!" she howled, slapping him. "Don't you know nothing about nothing? A strangler wouldn't have no knife in his hands, he'd have a pair of panty hose! Ain't you ever seen any strangler movies? Gawd!"

They were breaking up all over each other then, and when I went to bring the boyfriends' arm behind his back, I saw how gone the both of them were. The girl's eyes were red and spotty in the dim morning light, and the boy's body reeked of the stuff.

"Christ!" the boy hollered. "Don't yank my fucking arm off! We'll git, we'll git!"

The girl flashed a wounded look at the boy, as if he were the one who was forcing them to go, not me.

"I liked it here," she pouted, as they stood to leave. "There weren't any mosquiters, nor people, nor policemen. There weren't nothing here but us, and I liked it like that. Now we're gonna get caught in all this worthless rain."

I watched them as they weaved across the railroad tracks. When they had disappeared, I sat on the bench and rested.

"Your father is sleeping."

She sits at the kitchen table staring at the tablecloth. It is past twelve midnight, and her look is not one of weariness nor worry but the duty-ridden look of a woman who has been forced to stay up past her preference.

"Where have you been?"

"Out."

She runs her hand across the length of the tablecloth.

"Where you been out at?"

"Merreau Island."

"With who?"

"Nobody."

She gets up from the table and goes to the refrigerator and takes a swig of water from the waterjug. She looks at me and turns on the stovelight.

"What's her name?"

"Who?"

"Nobody. What's this Nobody-girl's name?"

"I don't know," I tell her. "Listen. What does it matter? I want to go to bed."

"All right," she says. She turns from the light. As I'm walking away she looks again and sees me scratching. "Wait."

"What."

My hand is beneath my arm, and I am digging at it, underneath my armpit.

"Why're you scratching there?"

I sigh at her.

"'Cause I got mosquito bit. Why else?"

"Don't be brief with me," she says. She holds my eyes in hers until I bow and look away. "You wait right here. And take off your shirt. I'm gonna get some calamine."

She leaves the room and I peel to my jeans. When she returns with the bottle she tells me to follow her into the utility room.

"And be quiet about it," she says. "I don't want to wake up your father."

We step carefully through the living room and into the utility and I sit on the washer with my hands on my knees. She dabs the lotion on a swab of cotton; then, for the first time, in the light of the overhead lamp, she takes me in fully.

"My Lord! Would you look at you?"

She stands there slack-jawed, staring, gaping.

"What? What is it, Mama? Hey? What is it?"

The piece of cotton falls from her hand. So does the bottle of calamine. It breaks with a quiet quick pop on the floor and I hear my father stirring on the couch in the next room.

"How old're you?" my mama asks.

She has not bent down to clean up the broken bottle and her look is still one of slow-thawing awe.

"Fourteen," I say.

Her head begins to nod.

"Fourteen," she repeats. "Yes. That's about right." She looks down at her hands. "How old was the girl you were with? Little Miss Nobody. How old was the girl? And don't lie."

"Sixteen," I tell her. "Maybe older. To tell you the truth, she never said."

"Sixteen," my mother says, soft, like an echo. "Sixteen. Yes. But then she never said."

We do not speak any for a short while. Then my mama shakes her head and bends down to the floor and smears her whole hand in the calamine puddle. She carries a look of satisfied disbelief on her face and holds up her hand like it's got a needle in it. The bright pink lotion runs rivers down her arm.

"What I should tell you to do is to strip yourself naked and wallow around in that calamine tarpit down there, and maybe it'll take the sting out of that mountain range of welts you got carved across your chest and back, and maybe it'll take the wang out of whatever other diseases you got fightin' for territory on the surface of your body. All I've got to say is the next time you go out with Nobody, you better make sure she's got a full bottle of insect repellent on her, and if she don't, you better have the sense to keep your nocturnal activities confined to the backseat of a car, or the canvas of a puptent, or wherever the hell else you let your sap drip these days. If there's one thing I'm sure of, it's that I'm too overworked to be tending a boy

with yellow fever, and you're too undernourished to have to be
thinking about a second mouth. And don't think you ain't old
enough to be playing dumb to what I'm saying, and don't you
stand there more hangmouth than me, acting like you don't
know what from what nor where it goes. Now turn your back,
Romeo, and when I'm gone take your dungarees off and do the
legs and the rest of you proper."

"Yes'm."

Then the calamine, cool, across my back, and the move-
ment of her hands around my neck and shoulderblades; and
when she has gone I take up a shard of glass from a broken
mirror in the corner of the utility room, and I study my body,
with its jigsaw patch of welts and pimples, and there is not a
part of me that is not dimpled—not chest, nor feet, nor face,
nor thighs: not even there; and I think to myself, "There ain't a
place that the insects haven't touched, not a piece of territory
that they cannot call their own." And I dress myself and begin
to itch, and when I enter the living room I see my father,
scratching himself in the crotch of his corduroys.

"You didn't have to pull that knife on them."

Walk fast to your own end. I'll be there to see you. Go.

I threw the knife in the ground, straight, like
mumbletypeg. Then I picked it up.

"No. I didn't."

I watch him hold it.

"See? Like this. Now!" He throws it; it goes in all the
way. "Ah! Right? Right? Ah, ha ha!"

I take the hilt in my hand and try it.

"No, no, no!"

He slaps me on the back of the head.

"More wrist," he says. "Look. One, two, three —snap!"

It drives in, farther than before. I pick it up for him, and
he has me try it again. When I am not throwing, we are drink-

*ing. When we are not drinking, I am throwing. It takes me one
night to learn it.*

"Here," he says. "To keep."

His knife is my knife.

"Stay put," I told him. "And don't move until I get
back."

He wandered around the rocks and stopped.

"You're going to get medicine, aren't you?"

I told him I was.

"You get medicine," he said. "And you won't come
back."

I looked at him. He sat amid all the white pebbles,
shoulders set real straight and solid, that bullheaded glaze
in his eyes. "What's with you, little professor?" He
jammed his hands down into his pockets like it was thirty
degrees below zero outside, and I saw the water starting
down his face. "Stop that," I said.

"Stop what?"

"You know," I told him. I ran a finger down my
cheek.

"I ain't stopping nothing," he told me, wiping the
tear hard and quick, like it was acid. "That was a raindrop.
I got hit in the face."

I looked at the sky and felt one on my back. The air
was all black and drawn back sort of ruffled, like a magi-
cian sweeping his cape. I felt two more drops on my head,
then three again on my back, then the whole sky commenced to falling.

"Ask that to stop," my brother said, laughing. "See if
you can do it," he told me, grinning cold.

*I'm lying in the lawn belly down on the grass, finger in
the slippery-round hole of the meter-reader. I feel it beneath*

me, the wet grass vibrating. Then she is behind me, hand around the mower throttle.

"Hey." She says my name. "Get on outta the way there."

I roll over a couple of yards where the grass isn't mowed. In a few minutes I feel her behind me, like before.

"Hey." She says my name again. "Listen, you. It's tough enough doing this with him dead out on the sofa. The least you can do is stay outta Mama's way."

I grin up, not budging.

"You want me to move you?"

We are on the knob of the slope at the front of our yard. With a push she could send me tumbling down.

"Come on, Mama. Gimme a good shove."

And she is laughing then, down on her knees, hands beneath my shirt all digging and pushing. She gives a giddy shout, and the world becomes a pinwheel, houses clinging to the sky and streetlights doing handstands and neighbors shooting up into space suspended by feet on warm-cement driveways.

"Awwwww, awwwww! Aw ha ha hawww!"

In the gutter, sweating, concrete against my stomach. There is grass on my elbows, mouth, thighs. When the mower moves away I can hear the women neighbors.

"Look at her doing that. In her condition? Where's the man responsible for her misery?"

"I heard her tell the little boy," says the other, not even looking at me, "that he's inside, watching the television. But if you as't me, he ain't inside. If you're talking about the father, why, he could be anywheres."

"Ah, yes," says her partner. "He could be acros't the state-line by now."

I leave them in their laughter and run to her. She kneels stooped in the shorn grass. She and it smell sweet.

"Help me with the catcher here."
I look at it and look at her. We lift.
"It's almost as big as you are."
She laughs.
"No. It's almost as big as you."
I touch her there and shrug at her.
"What I meant, Mama, was your stomach."

"Oh!" She lifts the bag higher and dumps it. "I ain't that
big." Her hands sift through the grass and pull out a few living
and chopped-up lizards. "And even if he were the same size,"
she says, taking one lizard and holding it before her face, so it
dances, "he ain't gonna dump so easy."

I ask her why she says "he."

"Because." She puts the lizard down on the lawn and it
runs in broken circles and juts out its neck and does calisthenics.
"I ain't bringin' another girl into this world."

I squat on the back of the carriage of the mower and she
rolls me to the backyard tool shed. When she has finished with
the mower she holds me by the arm and tells me to wait in the
shed while she closes the shed door. I do. In five minutes she
returns with the edger. Light floods the shed, and I can see her
shadow moving in orange smears toward me.

"Did you like that?"

She puts my hand against her, there.

"I know how he feels," I tell her, thinking: "Now I know
what he's going through."

The rain came down in bucket tosses, making its best
effort to drown the world on dry land. I could barely make
him out as he sat unmoving on his rockpile, looking like a
little boy anchored to the bottom of a public pool, cheeks
puffed and breath held stubborn, not much caring for the
commotion around him. There was lightning and the
noise of palms and terrific winds and clouds like stomachs

sagging, and the ground flinched and heaved undertoe
like an animal trying to shake you off its skin. I could feel
my chest going as the storm whipped up around us. I
wished it would swallow me so I could settle in the thick of
it, that there were palm fronds fastened to my forearms so
I could catch a quick zephyr and shoot straight up, that
there were some way I could breathe in the strength of the
storm and launch my body high above the stationary earth.
But there weren't no way.

"Listen!" I hollered. "You want to come with me?"

He brought his legs in tight around his body.

"What are you going to do?"

I looked at him, full, and said nothing. There certainly was some kind of a resemblance, in the nose and
hair and especially the eyes; even I had to admit it. It
must've been some fluke of Mother Nature. Somebody's
mother had to be to blame.

"I'm going to get some from the package store about
a quarter-mile from here. That's why you got to wait."

He buried his face, our face, in his hands.

"Grader on the green lumber! Grader on the green!"

*The foreman wears a ragged Cincinnati Reds cap and
waits by the moving belt with a pencil in his mouth. We watch
him through the chainlink fence as he stands bouncing slightly
on his heels.*

*"Grader on the green lumber! Grader on the green
lumber! Goddamn it, this green chain ain't gonna stop for no
man, even if he is determined to stop for it! Grader on the green
lumber! Grader on the green!"*

*A head pops out of the lumber office window. It is our
daddy, clean-shaven and grinning, craning his head sort of
backwards.*

"You hush your trap there, Charette!" he hollers. "That

wood ain't gonna get any greener, and my load ain't gonna dump any sooner! I shit off the clock anyway, so stop your yawping. Everything'll come out all right in the end!"

The pencil droops in the foreman's mouth and he trods off bowlegged while the other workers chuckle. A boom man in the log pond takes a spill and comes up soaked and laughing. He waggles his head like a wet St. Bernard and my daddy calls from the office window: "Thar she blows, mateys! Boom whale on the port bow! Har har har!"

I breathe in the sweet woody smell of the lumber and look at him beside me, hands around the chainlink.

"See?" I tell him. "Our daddy's a real popular guy."

He points to the conveyor where the foreman had stood. "Is that what Daddy does for a living?"

"Sure," I tell him. "He's a grader. He makes his living there."

From across the yard a toilet flushes. We hear a door slam and our daddy comes running across the lumber yard. He is dressed in bluejeans and a plaid flannel shirt and he wears a baseball cap with the name of a company or something or other written on it. He carries two long sticks in his hands, one with a hook on the end of it, the other with a crayon. He flips the moving lumber with the hook, looks the wood over good, scribbles on it with the crayon, and moves on to the next piece of lumber. He cannot see us waiting for him outside the fence and he works quickly and finishes most of the pieces on the conveyor belt, talking quietly to himself. "Grader on the green," he says in a nagging voice. "Grader on the goddamn green." When he finishes he turns and studies the fence and sees us and his face falls. He throws his sticks down at his side and makes a disappointed pretend-face. "Aw look, Doc," he says to someone who isn't beside him, "it's those no-good kids." He lets out a yell and comes charging the fence like a wildbull. We back away from

the chainlink laughing. With a single clutch and bound he is
over and has the both of us beneath his arms. "Teach you to
nose around my place of employment," he says, butting our
heads together. "Teach you to respect a working man,
punksticks." We all settle down, and he pushes me on the back
of the head and leads my little brother along by the hand. He
whistles, poorly, and we both walk slow so my brother doesn't
stumble.

"Where we meetin' your mother for lunch?" he asks.

"She says it's up to you, Daddy," I tell him. "But you
know what?"

He grins. His eyebrows arch. "What?"

"I bet she'd like to go to Snak City."

"Well!" he huffs, mulling it over. "I'd certainly go for
that!"

And he lifts my brother up in his arms, and we run racing
for the company lot.

"What you got to steal it with?" he asked, sounding
like me too, like I must've sounded when I was his age.

"My hands. And the knife, if I got to."

He did not look up.

"The man behind the counter's going to have more
than that."

"I know," I told him. "But he won't use it."

"He will if he sees you."

"He won't see me."

"He will if you pull that knife."

"I won't have to."

"What if you have to?"

"If I have to I'll run."

"And bullets run faster."

"And so do trains. And so do I."

His hair was plastered down around his forehead,

and he looked like something peeking out behind draperies. His face had that undefeated tilt to it, and he took up a palmful of pebbles and started dropping them down at his feet. He was the thinking type, all right. Twice as quick as me, it was the truth. If I'd lacked the will to let him make my decisions for me, I probably wouldn't have been in half the trouble I was in. But what good's a conscience if you let someone else go and ruin it for you?

"You comin' or what?"

"But the rain—" he began, and I had to laugh. As if the weather made any difference, as if a firestorm would've been reason enough to call the rest of it off. "No. Listen. You can go get the medicine afterwards, when the sky empties itself. I'll go with you after the storm."

"All right," I told him. "Pussy out. It don't matter none to me no more. I just better find you here when I get back."

As I rose to leave him in the switchyard house I could see in the distance the outline of the old bay bridge; it looked like the abandoned skin of a water moccasin. Already I could hear the whistle of another train a couple miles off, and I knew after that there'd be a third come twenty-five minutes, and a fourth following that. Because of the warnings I'd given him I didn't think my brother would have the courage to say my name again, but he did. I'd been walking away, but I turned back around and went to him and held him and struck him to the ground with my fist. He fell out of my arms and lay like a pile of bones scattered on the pebbles laughing. I told him to be quiet and wait in the switchhouse, but he wouldn't. He just kept laughing, real low, and saying my name over and over like he'd never heard nothing in the world so funny. I managed to get a good fifty yards away from him before I convinced myself that he needed checking up on, so I went back and found him stretched out rail to rail. He was laughing a little softer and saying just my last name now, like when you say a word to yourself and wonder how it came to get that word sound, and the more you say it the more awkward and hysterical it gets, until pretty soon it isn't even a word anymore, it's just a sound; and you can't bring yourself to remember what the sound stood for, or whether it stood for anything, really, and you feel your stomach tighten because nothing remains to distance you from the fear of what the word once meant.

I helped him over to the switchhouse and sat him down on the bench out of the rain. I realized that he wasn't laughing anymore. We sat there for a while and could hear ourselves dripping, and his throat made a struggling noise like something that wants air but has forgotten how to get it. After a while his breathing got back to regular and he said, "Where you going to put the medicine?"

I touched my pants pocket.

"Where'd you say?"

I touched my pants pocket again, and when he saw what I'd done his eyes went straight and narrow, like a bird's.

He ran a hand through his hair.

"I suppose," he said. "I suppose that's how it's got to be done."

Outside the shelter of the switchyard house it rained less heavy than before, the noise of it sounding something like fingers tapping music on a station wagon dashboard. I asked him if he wanted me to stay with him until he was all right again, and he said no, I could go about my business. I made him promise he'd wait until I got back, that he wouldn't lie beneath any more trains unless I was there to go about showing him the right way to do it.

He lay near-sleeping on a bench when I left him. His lower lip was broken from where I'd hit him, and you could see where one of his teeth was crooked and where the gumline was bloody and torn. It had been a long night for him. It had been a long one. The last thing he said to me before I left him on the bench was, "Walk fast to your own end. I'll be there to see you go." When he said it his voice was like paper tearing.

"Wake up."

"What?"

"Wake up and go to sleep."

He stretches his arms behind his neck and his eyes squinch up tight like somebody's blown salt in them. He looks at me with a reluctant smile and tries to shove the pillow over his head so he won't have to face me.

"You were doing it again," I tell him.

I pull the pillow away from him and he looks at me, blinking.

"Doin' what?"

I get up and close the door tight, so they can't hear.

"This," I tell him, and begin to sing. I finish, and he looks at me. "Just like that," I say. "Only you sung it twice as loud, and you kept your hands up around your mouth like you were trying to stop the words from coming out."

He looks at the door.

"Did they hear it?"

"No."

"Are you sure?"

"I ain't sure."

He rolls back over, face against the wall, not looking at me while he talks.

"Was it pretty? Hunh. I bet it was. You don't have to tell me it was 'cause I know."

After that I don't wake him in the nights when it happens. I just lie there and sometimes open the windows, listening to the music of the wind in the palms. He sings the same song every night, and he never sings it any time other than when he's in his bed sleeping, and sometimes I take my things to his room and lie there in the dark just waiting for him to begin, because it's the kind of thing you can go sleepless for, the kind of thing you can die feeling good you heard.

I took to the downslant of the pebble hill and it brought me to a clump of brush near the road. I could hear the skidding sounds of morning traffic, but I couldn't see anything of the street through the brush. The sky was getting slowly lighter and beneath me I could feel my own feet stumbling. But I felt strong in the legs, and the storm had perked my heart up some, and I knew that all I needed was a bottle of medicine to make everything complete.

Though there wasn't much rain falling, I was shivering from the dampness of the cold. I had to stop walking every couple of steps to let the chills run head to toe through me. I felt sorry being without anyone to walk with, and as I left the tracks for the brush I had the feeling that I might not make it without somebody to stick with, that if only I had some company, I could get through it all all right.

I came out of the trees and weeds and sandspurs and came upon a bunch of men working on a patch of road in the halflight. One had a rivet and the others had shovels and they were all dressed in seethrough rainslickers, even though it was raining so light there wasn't any need for them. None of the men had much to say to each other and they went about their work in hangdog silence. I tried to pass by one guy in a necktie who sat sort of sullen on a bleached barricade, and he punched me lightly on the shoulder.

"You know how to break road?" he said. "One of our men done quit on us. I'll give you twenty-five dollars straight out of my pocket if you break road for my crew for five and a half hours. That's as good a pay as any of these men are getting, and I can see you're strong enough to do the work."

I looked at the other workers and they were taking me in sort of lethal and hard, like I might be a potential traitor. I turned on the man in the necktie.

"I don't want any part of your business," I told him. "Not for twenty-five dollars or twenty-five hundred."

I hadn't gotten more than a block away when I heard the sound of running behind me. It was a worker stooped over in his rainslicker, and he had something lumped in his hand which he wanted me to take. I asked him what it was, and he said it was money. I told him I didn't need it because what I wanted I could steal, and he said he supposed I'd make a manager some day.

"I hear tell you're taking applications for stockboys."

He sticks his gum behind his ear and pulls a piece of wax from the other one.

"How old're you, son?"

"Eighteen."

"Eighteen, huh? You be straight with me now."

"I'm eighteen, sir," I tell him, trying to make my voice drop. "I swear it in truth."

"Well," he says, squinting an eye, "if y'are eighteen, and not merely in talk, take this form and fill it out. You have a pen?"

"No, sir, I—"

"Here." He reaches beneath the counter and tosses me a ballpoint. "Fill it out and give it to the head cashier."

"Thank you, sir. I will."

I leave the store and look for him. He sits at a busstop bench bouncing a Super Ball in between his knees. I settle beside him and snatch the ball away and he stares at the form I got folded in my hands.

"You want me to fill it out?" he asks.

I nod yes.

There wasn't much to speak of as far as the streets surrounding the old bay port were concerned, just a couple of fruit stands, an auto parts store, half a dozen bars, and as many big churches. To get to where I had to go I took a shortcut through a parking lot where tool sheds of all different shapes and sizes were displayed for folks to look at. Obviously someone had forgotten to lock the sheds up the night before, because as I walked through the lot I could hear derelicts and portbums snoring and talking to themselves from inside the sheds. As I came to the last and biggest shed on the lot—a light blue number with pink-and-yellow daffodil trimmings—I opened the swinging doors to find a dozen bums lumped together on the floor. Their clothes were worn and ratty, and their hair was greasy and rank, and one of them scooted over to make room for me on the floor. "Plenty of room for everybody," he said. Another one, who looked like he might have been sleeping before I barged in, stared up at me with unbelieving sheephead eyes and asked if it had stopped storming. I told him it had.

"Ma'am?"

"Uh-huh."

"Manager told me to give this to you."

She takes the application and surveys it.

"Why, all right. I'd be glad to take this for you. I'll give it right back to the hiring man and if he's interested he'll give you a call before the week's out."

When I leave, the cashier lady tells me I have pretty handwriting. I thank her and give my brother an extra quarter.

The tool shed lot led to a muddy gravel road that looped back in a halfcircle to the parking lot of an old church. The parking lot lay on low-lying ground and had flooded over with rainwater from the morning storm. A bunch of kids were out early playing in the flooded still-water, little boys and girls with shirts off and water to their waists, splashing each other and dunking one another and shooting jets of water from puckered blowfish mouths. One older kid on a streetbike came tearing through the flooded lot with a little girl on a roped-up skimboard sitting behind him. The wooden board cut a zigzag pattern through the filthy water, and the little girl knelt with her hands around the plank, laughing and hollering, "Faster! Faster!" When the older boy got tired he dropped his bike on the less wet grass and took the skimboard and ran at the shallower water with it. He'd get going real fast, then drop the board and hop on top of it, and a couple of times he got out of control and flipped head over heels from the slippery wood. The little girl, who I supposed was his sister, clapped her hands and hugged herself every time the boy had an accident, and once he took such an awful spill that he rose from the water with his forehead bleeding. He wasn't hurt bad, just bloodied up, and his sister ran at him squeezing her hands.

She jumped on him and started to pet him, as if to tell all the other kids this hero was her brother, his blood was partially hers, and the boy seemed to take a liking to the little girl's fawning. He lifted her high up over his head and spun her around twice for good measure, then brought her down butt first in the skanky water. She came up gagging and laughing, and as soon as she'd caught her breath she threw herself on top of him again and tried to force him under the water. To be a good sport he let her have her way, and down he went, her small body bobbing on his shoulders.

I went to them.

"Did you ever pour water over me like him?"

Beside the basin, a cup of his hands.

"Did you ever pour water over me like him?"

She takes, he lifts, they let the water trickle.

"Did you ever pour water over me like him?"

The name, him crying, they pronounce together.

"Did you ever pour water over me like him?"

And they say, "No." And it is not a lie.

"Do me."

The boy looked me over funny.

"Do me," I told him.

I knelt down in the water.

"What do you mean?" he said.

He did not move.

"Do me," I repeated.

He was about my age.

His sister stopped splashing and went to his side.

"See?" she whispered. "He wants to be baptized."

The boy broke out into a mean peal of laughter.

"Goddamn! Me? Oh, goddamn!"

The little girl told him to be quiet.

"Don't say 'goddamn' if'n you got to baptize!"

"Baptize!" he howled. "I ain't no goddamn priest."

She said he didn't have to be.

"Hell," he told her. "I ain't even celebrate!"

She asked him what him that meant, and he moved his hand like he was jacking off.

"Stop it," she said.

He told her to be quiet. Then he looked at me and gave me a kick and said, "Get up!"

I told him I wouldn't.

"Do me," I said. "I come here. It's only right, and you got to."

"Got to!" he snorted. "I ain't got to do nothing! And if you want to kneel up to your neck in shitwater, that's up to you. Come on, Dolores."

His sister looked at me pitifully and the two of them made to leave. I noticed then that all the other children had gathered close around us. It was impossible for the boy to get out of his duty.

"Do me," I repeated, and he turned around and started toward me. "Now you ain't got no other way."

When the boy's face was about five inches from mine he said, "All right. I'll do you." And he struck me in the jaw and his boot rammed up into the crotch of my pants and there came a noise of splashing and screaming and running. I rose from the water to find that all the children and the boy and girl had gone, and though my groin ached and my mouth was running, it was a baptism of sorts and I felt somehow better.

"Did you ever pour water over me like him?"

I limped from the lot to the church courtyard.

Walk fast to your own end. I'll be there to see you. Go.

I was bloody from being hit and pretty dirtied up by

the stillwater and I knew I couldn't get medicine unless I'd cleaned myself a bit. I looked around the churchyard for a water spigot but couldn't find none, so I tried the door of the church, and it was open. It was a good thing for me there wasn't nobody inside, 'cause I knew there had to be something wrong about what I was doing; I didn't want to run the risk of getting in trouble with the law when I'd come as far as the morning had brought me.

First thing, when I entered the church, I found a bowl of water attached to the wall beside the door. It was cold and it had a sweet, perfumish smell to it, and I took it out and dumped it over my neck and chest and shoulders. I found two more waterbowls just like it and did the same with them, but I knew I wasn't clean yet, so I wandered about the church looking for more. I tried to keep my head down because I knew if I looked at all the things in the church, I'd either feel guilty and leave or get so taken in by the prettiness of it all I wouldn't want to finish what it was I had to do. Now and then, just to indulge myself a little, I took a peek at the tiny framed pictures they had on the sidewalls every couple of pews. I didn't look at the stained glass none because I knew it was too nice for me to set my eyes on. I just concentrated instead on the pictures of the suffering man, because they were so plain and simple drawn I figured they mustn't have been too important.

The pictures started on the right-hand side of the church and followed all the way around to the very end of the left-hand side. There were about fourteen cartoon frames in all, and only after I'd studied the first five did I come to understand that a story was being told.

In the first episode you saw two guys taking the suffering man out of what looked like some kind of bathtub where he must've been soaking. He was awfully punk and sickly-looking, and the men had him wrapped in a towel so he wouldn't be naked.

In the second episode you saw the same two fellas trying to get the suffering man to stand up, he was so pitiful weak and everything. They had him leaning against some kind of healing cross, and you could tell that if they could only get the poor guy up there, he might start coming around to himself.

Episode three had him up there all right, but he didn't look no better. His eyes were still closed and that dead heaviness hung about his face. A man and a woman, probably his mama and daddy, had gathered beneath the healing cross praying for him to come to, but they didn't look too hopeful.

Number four was less bleak than the first three because at last the suffering man had come around. His eyes were wide open and he was moaning in agony while the physician's assistants helped him off the cross. One of the men steadied him while the other drew the surgical-steel bolts from out of his hands and feet, and I was surprised that neither of the men took that heavy-looking solid-gold helmet from off the suffering man's head. Maybe it was part of his continuing treatment; I didn't know. But it certainly looked uncomfortable.

Come the fifth episode the suffering man was getting downhome service. Two soldiers had gotten him a new set of clothes and they were helping him try them on. The stuff looked like it fit him pretty good, but the suffering man wore this burnt-cheese expression, as if their tastes clashed.

Episode six had the suffering man down on the ground, like he'd fallen from the weight of the new clothes or what-have-you. The soldiers looked annoyed that he couldn't handle a new set of skivvies, and they were bending down to help him to his feet.

In the seventh picture the suffering man seemed to have made a lightning recovery. He had his healing cross tucked under his arm and he was asking some ladies the quickest way to get back home. They were crying and sobbing because they couldn't help him none and his cross looked awful heavy, but he seemed to be saying to the women, "Cool your jets, now. This here thing looks heavy, but it'll make me whole again. You should've seen how weak I was till I got this thing. Don't let looks deceive you; this here cross is the living end."

Episode eight was sort of funny and I got a bang out of it because it was so true. Right after you mouth off to somebody about how you're on the road to recovery, how you never felt stronger or better in health, straight out of nowhere comes absolute trouble. Number eight showed you the suffering man on the ground a second time, only minutes after he'd bragged to the crying ladies about his journey and his healing cross. And who was helping the suffering man now? Who else but the same beleaguered soldiers. They must have been sick to death of tending him.

The ninth episode was awful strange and I wasn't sure I understood it, but it was real beautiful and mysterious and I spent the longest time just studying it. It seemed as if the suffering man had run into this artist girl who was trying to make some kind of Xerox copy of his face with a veil. I didn't know what she put on the veil to get it there, but she certainly did one hell of a job. When the suffering man pressed his face down onto it, a second, identical face bloomed up. I supposed the girl gave the veil to him as a keepsake, because in the tenth episode it was plain that while one man was helping him carry his healing cross, two other dudes—I tried to convince myself that they weren't the pair of soldiers—were busy trying to hustle the veil out of the suffering man's backpocket. For all I knew they might have done it too; the next episode didn't say.

Episode eleven showed the suffering man asking directions from another lady. Just like the other women, she didn't have any idea where he should go, but she prayed for him and cried over him and he went on his way, only to fall down a third and final time in the twelfth episode. It was a good thing for the suffering man that the two soldiers were there to help him. They must have been trailing him a good while suspecting he might need their help, and being regular princes they lifted him up and pointed him in the right direction.

In episode thirteen the soldiers had gotten the right idea about how to care for the suffering man. They tied a rope around him so he wouldn't stray or collapse anymore, and they pushed him onward with his healing cross in the direction of his home.

Episode fourteen, the final picture, saw the suffering man reunited with his loved ones, with the soldiers commencing to untie the rope. It was an inspiring sight seeing the suffering man having come so far—from sickness to health, from loneliness to good company, from being lost to being found—and it did a heart good to study that picture because it was just like the way life should be. You almost felt as if you'd gone all the way from death to life with him, and I wanted to walk on over to the right side of the church and start the journey all over again, but I knew I couldn't. Time was wasting, and I needed to clean myself.

I scavenged around the front of the church and came upon a gold basin full of all the water I could possibly need. I lifted off the top of the contraption and took a step up with the intention of getting in, but I realized that I might get stuck, it being so small and everything, so I contented myself with dunking my head under and came up feeling wet and dizzy as a dog.

"I saw this thing, a new thing. Girl showed it to me at school."

He drops his booksack on the hallway floor and runs to the bathroom. I follow him, and he kneels in front of the toilet.

"What? You gonna throw up or something? Some girl teach you how to throw up?"

He rolls his eyes.

"No, no. I know how to throw up."

I pat him on the back.

"Right proud of you there."

"Come off it," he says. He rolls up his shirtsleeves and unbuttons his collar and brushes his hair back off his forehead. His eyes are hysterical and excited-looking. "She showed me something else," he says. "A neat trick." Next thing I know he has his hand over his nose and his head in the toilet. His other hand gropes for the flusher and he catches it and pulls and begins to holler with laughter. When he rises from the throne his hair stands in a Dippity-Do, like the top of a soft-serve ice-cream cone. "Swirly! Swirly! She taught me how to get a Swirly!"

Without warning I take him by the neck and shove his head in the toilet. I flush it about five million times, just to keep him from growing up a geek. When he comes up he barely breathes.

"Serves you right," I tell him. "You can't go around shoving your head in toilets."

"But the girl—" he chokes. *"And it was funny! And I thought you'd—"*

Not listening, I leave him there. He kneels before the john, choking and crying, looking into the john-hole like a man who's lost his heart. That night, when I go to bed, I wake to find a candy-bar turd steaming beneath my feather pillow.

I left the church.

Walk fast to your own end.

Past the churchyard the package store stood.

I'll be there to see you.

I went to it, sprinting, feeling my blood.

Go.

A small Vietnamese woman stood behind the counter. She was young and wore a starched denim dress and had a face that told you how poor she slept. Her hair was long and dimly black and fell in two sickles across her chest and stomach. Behind her on the counter a baby lay sleeping in a worn wicker basket, and beside it a ghetto blaster played rock 'n' roll for the child to sleep to. The woman looked me over with curious silver-blue shooting marble eyes and didn't seem to mind that I couldn't stop staring at her. She grinned and swallowed and ran her fingers across her dress and asked me why I didn't have my shirt on. I told her I took it off because it was hot.

"Hot," she nodded, smiling, "yes. It very wahm. It rain, too." She lifted her hands up over her head and made her fingers flutter. "Like dis, ah hah."

The baby stirred behind her and she went to it and picked it up.

"He lock stohm, dis one!"

She shook the baby and he began to cry. She stroked him.

"I like storms too," I told her.

"Ah hah," she nodded. "Pretty noisy!"

When she went to put the baby back down I reached beneath the counter and grabbed a flask of anything. I put it in the pocket of my pants and could feel it pressing against my leg.

The woman said, "Husband out. Backyahd. You wait fah heem, else I hep you."

I told her no, I didn't want anything; I just came in to get out of the storm.

"He still stohm?" she asked.

"No," I told her. "It's over, for now. But it'll start up again."

She turned back around from the baby and nodded. "Ah, yes, like dis." She made her hands dance.

"Yes," I told her. "Uh-huh. Just like that."

We were quiet for a moment, and I made no move to go. As long as she was facing me I was afraid if I left she might see the bulging bottle. So I stood there, playing the idiot, and asked her how old her child was. "Siss months," she said, and changed the subject. She reached for a package of sugar wafers and held them up before me. "You hungry? You have eaten? I give you dis, if you wont."

Before I could refuse she laughed and threw them at me.

"Cookies! Jus' cookies! You pay back when you got dis." She held her hand out and rubbed her fingers together.

I took the package and held it over my pocket.

"Thank you, ma'am. Thank you very much."

I blushed and fawned and turned to go, the cookies in my hand covering the pocket of my pants, but as soon as we'd said goodbye I heard her draw her breath.

"Wot that?" she said. "In yo' pocket?" She pointed

her finger at my pantsleg, angrily, and her shoulders were jerking. "That? Wot that there? You puh eet bahk, p'ease!"

She was not screaming or anything, just mad as hell, and I didn't want to hurt or frighten her any. I put my finger slowly over my lips and with my other hand drew out the knife. She stopped shaking.

"Look," I told her. I pointed the knife out at her. "You take it. A trade."

"Nah!" she said, furiously, folding her arms down hard across her chest. "You puh eet bahk rot now, p'ease!"

I told her I couldn't.

She looked at me.

"I call husband!"

"No," I begged. "Please."

To show her I didn't mean no harm, I went to the counter and laid the knife on it. She picked it up and her face blanched—she must've felt some of the blood. She walked calmly to the register and put the knife in it. Her hands rummaged around for something in the back of the cash drawer.

"You puh bahk," she repeated.

I told her again I couldn't.

"You puh bahk."

Her hands kept moving and her eyes were full.

"You puh bahk goddamn rot now!"

She did not point the gun at me but kept it at her side. Inside the store all was silent. The baby had fallen back to sleep and the radio sang gently. All I could hear was the soft breathing noise of the morning outside. I had begun to suspect that the woman's husband wasn't there, that she'd only said it as a protection of sorts, and I could see that she was terrified. I did not look at the gun in her hand, and I nodded my head at the backdoor of the store. I shoved a second flask in my free pocket and smiled.

"Call your husband."

She looked at me.

"Call your husband."

I took out the second flask and let it shatter on the floor.

"Call him," I repeated, and she began to cry.

She lifted the pistol slowly from her side, using the strength of both hands to raise it. It was the funniest thing. From where I stood, her arm looked like it wasn't the thing that was doing the lifting. It was almost as if there were an invisible rope bolted to the package store ceiling, some pulley and chain and unseen hand was hefting to get her to put the gun up at me. I kept looking at her elbow, and it seemed to fight gravity, and her wrist and all her white clenched fingers trembled with some type of terrible weight. When she spoke her voice had a hollow ring to it, as if she'd stepped out of herself or someone else had stepped on in. To do what she had to do, it was clear that someone beside herself had to do it, someone with or without a strength or weakness she usually had or lacked.

"Out," she told me.

I moved toward her.

"P'ease," she said, gun pointed straight.

"Call your husband," I told her, approaching. "Call him if we ain't got nobody but ourselves."

I remembered staring at the hole of her mouth as I crossed the floor to her. It did not call for help, or beg a man's name, or ask any favor. It remained open, slightly, taking in whatever air the small room had to offer, repeating what looked like an unspoken "no" in one-two-three succession. There wasn't any husband. He'd either died or had left her or had gone off for the morning; he wasn't in the backyard nor nowhere nearby, and even if he had been, he was far beyond her rescue. By the look on her face I could tell she had next to no one.

"Listen," I whispered.

Before I went behind the counter toward her, I told her I was going to hang the "Closed" sign up so nobody would come in. I also told her I was going to lock the door in case someone tried to. That was when the noise of her crying stopped. She said "No" once, aloud and wearily, and pointed the gun at the child in the basket. It did nothing; it could not move.

"Put it down! Put it down! Oh God, put it down!"
He is crying below it and maybe I should feed him.
"Put it down! Put it down! Oh God, put it down!"
He gathers me up and he carries me home.
"Put it down! Put it down! Oh God, put it down!"
Hold me under forever then. Never let me up.
"Put it down. Please. Oh God, put it down."

And the baby not stirring as she moved it from its forehead.

"Now, you go."
"I'll go, now."
I'll be there to see you.
Go.

The stench of the stillborn raindead sky and the sound of my flight as I fled the package store and the pressure of the bottle in my pocket on my thigh and a knowledge that the death of all living had begun to unravel like string in a young boy's pocket to collapse like a puppet given scissors and a will to undo itself like hope or the ticking of a clock or the rhythm of the heart beneath the prodding of a knife I thought—

Go.
Past the package store.
Go.
Through the churchyard.
Go.
Past the shelter sheds.
Go.
Through the slickermen.
Walk fast to your own end. I'll be there to see you.

Going swiftly up the hill I saw a set of soiled clothes, and next to it the mask of a criminal, suffering face of a newsprint fugitive. I could've stopped to pick it up, but the tracks felt slick and the voice said *Go* and faraway I saw the roof and the stoop-shouldered shape of him waiting there.

And I thought to myself, "He has blood written on him."

And I thought to myself, "It is what I can read."

And the sky tore in two like the skin of a balloon and I saw him rise and start to run then slow and walk not quickly even. He could see me, halfbrother, falling in the halflight, calling his name in the bleeding of the rain. He could hear, from where he stood, the screaming of the bottle, and see the blood and medicine spread outward on my leg.

Walk fast to your own end. I'll be there to see you. Go.

And see the blood and medicine spread outward on my leg.

He lay on his back bleeding from his thigh.

I took his arm and dragged him from the tracks so the train wouldn't get him. He had a face like an empty jar and he screamed when I reached into his pocket to take the glass out. I had to leave one piece in because it was too deep for me to remove, and whenever I'd try for it he'd cringe and holler and curse the names of our father and mother. I figured he'd be weak soon enough so I could get it then, and I asked him if he was suffering.

"Man," he said. "It don't scare me none."

I asked him what it was that didn't scare him any.

"You know," he said. "Blood. Bones. I got medicine now so it don't scare me."

I looked at him and told him it should and he tried to stand and fainted. In the rain the blood ran through his pants like peaked watercolors, and when he awoke I sat on the rail while he watched me. I took off one shoe, rolled the sock down from my knee, and put them both beneath his head for a pillow. His eyes drifted like two dead leaves in altogether different directions.

He said, "I'm leaving now."

"So long."

He bit his lip.

"If you come after me—" he threatened, and started to laugh.

I rose from the hill and went to the switchhouse. I looked about for something to cover him with. The rain was light and rapid and warm, but though it seemed to wash him clean it didn't keep the heat going well through his body. I found a black tarpaulin in the corner of a corridor and I took it up and shook it out and brought it over to him.

"Here," I said. I draped it across him.

He nodded his head and the chills began to take. I couldn't see any more of the blood except for that which ran a river down the white pebble hill, and when his body had stopped shaking I asked him if he wanted me to move him to the switchhouse.

"No," he told me. He asked me to turn the tarpaulin.

I rose and turned it and watched it flutter down. The belly-up side looked like a skinned animal, and it smelled of the sweetness that new blood smells of. I waved at the bugs that had clotted his wound.

"Move," he told me, twitching beneath the tarp. "Move," he repeated. "Move the rocks away."

I lifted his back as best I could and tried to sweep the pebbles from beneath his body, but there were too many and they ran too deep.

"It's a hill of stone," I told him. "No matter how far you dig you can't get nothing else."

My brother brought his hand, then, slowly to his face. He pressed his fingers to his eyes and I saw the glint of new-pulled glass between his thumb and palm. "Liar," he whispered, holding his breath; and the blood began to pour. It ran beneath the tarp like a dead red river and spilled across the rocks like wine from a broken cup. As I knelt beside his body taking in his eyes, I felt it wetting my feet and hands, and when his face and the arch of his chest had fallen, I left him on the hill and went up to the tracks.

I could hear them laughing as I lay across the rails. One was the pregnant girl who'd made fun of the waterspouts. The other was the younger one who'd chased her across the old port barge. They were dressed in summer dresses and moved idly through the weeds, and they did not stop to watch my brother bleeding on the hillside. They moved onward, simply, as if they had somewhere to go, and their laughter followed me down into the darkness where I knew it would not be long, nor uneasy, nor anything other than what I had to finish.

From where I lay I could see my brother. He was broken, and bleeding, and wore my father's features.

I was dead set against him going, but there was nothing I could do.

A NOTE ABOUT THE AUTHOR

Daniel Vilmure was born in Tampa,
Florida, in 1965, and graduated from
Harvard. *Life in the Land of the Living* is
his first novel.

A NOTE ON THE TYPE

This book was set in Granjon, a type
named in compliment to Robert Granjon,
type cutter and printer, active in Antwerp,
Lyons, Rome, and Paris from 1523–1590.
The face was designed by George W. Jones,
who based his drawings on a type used by
Claude Garamond (c. 1480–1561).

Composed by
Adroit Graphic Composition Inc.,
New York, New York

Printed and bound by Fairfield Graphics,
Fairfield, Pennsylvania

Designed by Marysarah Quinn